**OPERATOR 5:
THE COMING OF THE MONGOL HORDES**

THE COMING OF THE MONGOL HORDES

By Curtis Steele

POPULAR PUBLICATIONS • 2022

© 1938, 2022 Argosy Communications, Inc. All rights reserved.
Authorized and produced under license.

PUBLISHING HISTORY

"The Coming of the Mongol Hordes" originally appeared in the January/February, 1938 (Vol. 10, No. 1) issue of *Operator #5* magazine. Copyright © 2022 by Argosy Communications, Inc. All rights reserved.

ALL RIGHTS RESERVED

No part of this book may be reproduced or utilized in any form or by any means, electronic or mechanical, without permission in writing from the publisher.

This edition has been marked via subtle changes, so anyone who reprints from this collection is committing a violation of copyright.

Visit POPULARPUBLICATIONS.COM for more books like this.

CHAPTER 1
TROPHIES FOR THE VANDALS

THIS WAS enemy country to the two Americans who now crept so carefully through the burned Pennsylvania cornfield, toward the little village that lay in spreading ruins down the side of the hill. A detail of Mongolian riflemen were riding, at that very moment, into the village from the west. Those Mongols rode in loose formation, rifles under their arms. Strapped to the saddlebags of each trooper were various objects of loot, seized in other towns on the line of march.

The setting sun occasionally glinted on a more grisly object than loot. For many carried, tied to their pommels, the severed head of an American woman, attached by the hair.

The vast armies of the Purple Empire had passed this way. Here, men had fought and died, and the Purple Empire had set its mailed fist over America, as it had ruled the rest of the world. For two years had followed the reign of fire, sword and headsman's ax.... Now, America had broken the grip of Rudolph I. But the Mongol divisions of that ravaging conqueror's armies, a quarter of a million strong, had struck out for themselves, and established their own over-lordship upon all territory from the Great Lakes almost to the doors of Philadelphia.

THE TWO Americans in the cornfield watched the enemy detail with set faces and bleak eyes. There was still enough light so that there could be no mistake about the nature of those

OPERATOR 5

Operator 5 fired, sighting at the catapult's Mongol guard, a thousand yards away!

bloody trophies carried by the Mongols. One of those severed heads was attached to the pommel of the leader, a squat, flat-headed sergeant. With each step of the sergeant's horse, the head bounced up and down, dripping blood. It hung from two long braids of flaxen hair, and the dead features were twisted into a horrible travesty of what had been, only a little while before, the face of a beautiful woman.

The two American scouts remained very still in the cornfield,

THE COMING OF THE MONGOL HORDES

squatting on their haunches, rifles ready, in event of discovery. One was a young man in the uniform of an American captain of Intelligence. The other was a boy, yet tall, lithe, keen-eyed. The leaders of the Mongol horde to the west would have paid more for the heads of these two than for the capture of a whole American army.

The young man in the captain's uniform had, almost single-handed, prevented the Purple Empire from obtaining a firmer grip upon the country. To his friends, he was known as Jimmy Christopher. But in the archives of the United States Intelligence Service—a service now as defunct as the very Government of the United States—he was Operator 5. It was Operator 5's military strategy which had broken the backbone of the Purple armies at the Battle of the Continental Divide, only a few months ago.

The boy at his side was a lad whom Operator 5 had taken under his wing, trained into an able, efficient assistant. He had taken Tim Donovan into tight places where he would have hesitated to take a grown man; the two had become inseparable.

The boy, his pert young Irish face overcast with horror, was studying the Mongol column through field glasses.

"Look, Jimmy," he said hoarsely, "I can count fifteen heads tied to their pommels. From the appearance of them, they must be fresh victims!"

Jimmy Christopher nodded somberly, bitterness in his voice. "General Shan Hi Mung knows how to keep his troops happy. Hundreds of American women are paying with their heads to keep those Mongols in good spirits!"

He pushed forward, cautiously, through the corn, Tim close behind.

THE ENEMY column was riding swiftly into the town below them, spurring horses madly now, and waving bayonets high in the air to the accompaniment of blood-curdling yells.

Within the town, itself, some fifty or sixty women and children and old men came running out of the crumbling ruins in

THE COMING OF THE MONGOL HORDES

which they had taken shelter from the intense cold. These were American refugees who had originally lived here, prior to the Purple Invasion two years ago, and since returned to the site of their old homes to attempt to reconstruct a new life out of the ruins.

All over America this task of reconstruction was going on—an undertaking rendered all the more difficult by the lack of building facilities. Two years of war had destroyed the resources of a once prosperous and industrious country. There were no powerhouses to furnish electric light, wells to furnish oil, or mines for coal. Everything which had contributed to the cultured civilization, resulting from centuries of progress, had been wiped out in two years.

These people, now returning to their old homes, were pioneers as had been their forefathers. They possessed only raw primitive material with which to work with, and, in addition, were under the ever-present threat of Purple raiding parties.

Tim Donovan pushed up close to Operator 5, still peering through his glasses. "Those women and children won't have a chance to escape, Jimmy. The Mongols will ride them down. Look!"

The enemy horsemen were charging down the debris-littered main street, spreading out into two columns so as to surround the refugees. The women huddled close together, pressing young ones to their breasts, while the old men, many of them cripples, raised sticks, clubs, old rusty rifles in defense against the marauders.

The Mongols swirled around the pitiful group, riding in an

ever-narrowing circle, until within striking distance. Then their wickedly gleaming bayonets darted in and out in swift, deadly thrusts, smashing down the feeble resistance of the old men.

Cold steel pierced old and battered bodies, and the aged defenders went down in a welter of blood, to be trampled under the hooves of the Mongols' horses.

Shrill screams tore through the air, rising to the ears of Operator 5 and Tim Donovan, on the hillside. The Mongols had dismounted, sliding their rifles into the scabbards of their saddles. In place of the rifles, they drew their short, wide-bladed sabers, and rushed upon the women.

Tim Donovan uttered a cry of rage, and started to raise his rifle. But Operator 5's iron hand clamped down upon his wrist, forcing him to lower the weapon.

"Tim! If you fire a single shot, I swear I'll kill you!" His glare was steady now.

The young Irish lad gaped at him, wide-eyed. "B-but, Jimmy—they're going to behead those women and children. They'll tie their heads on the saddles!"

Operator 5's jaw muscles were set. When he finally spoke, his voice was stern. "We've got a job to do, Tim. We must find out why the Mongols were able to capture and destroy the five blockhouses encountered on their march east. So far, not a word has reached us as to what actually happened. We know they have no cannon, any more than we have. They have no planes or bombs that could have been dropped on the blockhouses. Yet, here they are, marching to New York. If we don't discover their

THE COMING OF THE MONGOL HORDES

secret, New York is as good as lost. We can't let anything stop us from moving west till we learn that secret."

He paused, watching the fracas below. The Mongols were snatching the children from their mothers, herding them together, while they dragged the women into a separate group. Many of the troopers were whetting their sabers, licking their lips at the prospect of bloody diversion before them. The bodies of the old men, whom they had slaughtered, lay disregarded under their feet.

Operator 5 kept his eyes on that scene, and forced himself to say, "Tim, our real mission comes first. *We've got to let them die!*"

The knuckles of Tim Donovan's small hands whitened with the intensity of their grip upon his rifle. His freckled cheeks flushed with high indignation.

"Jimmy, you can't do it! Those women are Americans. Their men are fighting for our country. *You can't* let them down." The boy moved up close to Operator 5, put an imploring hand on his shoulder. "No matter what our job is, Jimmy, we can't stand here and let those women be slaughtered. Suppose your sweetheart—Diane—were among them, or your sister, Nan? Would you take it as coolly? Look, they're dragging those women toward the cellars! Do you know what they're going to do to them down there, before they behead them?"

Operator 5 shook off the boy's hand, and swung to face him. His mouth was twisted into a tight line of despair; and there was that in his eyes that made Tim Donovan gulp.

"Don't say any more, Tim." His voice was cold, almost toneless, taut from terrible restraint. "Do you think I'm taking this coolly? If you think that, then you haven't learned to know me in the last three years."

Suddenly contrition assailed Tim. His eyes filmed. "I'm sorry, Jimmy," he said quickly. "I—I didn't think." He was remembering other times, when Operator 5 had risked his life in reckless undertakings to rescue Americans from the cruelty of the Purple troops—of times when Operator 5 and he had snatched victims from the very shadow of the headman's ax. "You must be burning up inside, the way I am. Only, I haven't got the guts to stick to the job. It would be so much easier to pile into this crowd and take a fling at saving those women, than to see them die. I…" he gulped hard. "Let's be going, Jimmy!"

Operator 5 nodded. "Let's go. We can skirt this field, and hit the Lancaster road without attracting the attention of those Mongols."

HE TURNED to the left, and led the way, crouching, toward the west, moving at an angle so as to come out on the road far west of the town. As he crawled forward, he spoke over his shoulder, talking as if he felt the need of justifying himself. "Thousands of Americans have died for the country in the last two years, Tim—and they've died uselessly. Those women down there would want to die rather than be saved, if they knew that the price of saving them would be the loss of the chance to unearth the secret of the Mongols' successful advance. I swear to you, Tim, that if Diane or Nan were down there with them, I'd leave them!"

Tim, close behind him, breathed, "I believe you, Jimmy."

THEY MOVED on in silence now, advancing with agoniz-

THE COMING OF THE MONGOL HORDES

ing slowness. In the town below, they could see the Mongol raiders bunching the children, who numbered some ten or twelve, in a close group up against a partially destroyed wall. Half a dozen troopers faced the frightened, crying children. They sheathed their sabers, went to their horses and got out rifles.

Both Operator 5 and Tim Donovan knew what that meant.

Down the street, another dozen of the Mongol troopers were dragging the women toward cellars and shell holes. Even as the two American scouts watched, one of the troopers, whose thick hand was wrapped in a woman's golden hair, turned and ripped the dress from her body. Then he wrapped his arms around her, carrying her in the direction of a house whose four walls were still standing, but without a roof.

The golden-haired woman screamed once, and began to kick and claw. The trooper struck her full in the face with the back of his hand, choking the scream in her throat. He disappeared with his burden into the house.

The riflemen had returned now, lining up some fifty feet from the huddled group of children.

Tim Donovan stopped, gazing back at the scene with clenched fists. He threw a swift glance at Operator 5's back, a few feet ahead of him. He started to speak, then choked back the words. He knew the importance of the mission upon which they were traveling in enemy territory. Four weeks ago, a Mongol army, under the Purple General, Shan Hi Mung, had captured Chicago, forcing the Continental Congress, assembled there, to flee. Two hundred and fifty thousand strong, they had begun to march east, with the avowed intention of joining forces with the Purple High Fleet under Admiral von der Selz, and capturing New York.

Six blockhouses had been hastily erected in the line of their march, and manned with all the American volunteer troops available in the territory. In the meantime, another force was fortifying Valley Forge, which would be the last strong defense before New York itself. The blockhouses had been intended only to slow up the advance of the Mongols until Valley Forge could be adequately fortified; but the Mongols had not been slowed up at all. Reports began to come in, showing Shan Hi Mung's troops to be moving east at a pace which meant that none of those six blockhouses had constituted any sort of obstacle.

It became obvious that the Mongols must have developed some type of war machine capable of demolishing the primitive blockhouses reared by the Americans. If that were the case, then the Valley Forge defenses would not stop them, either, and New York must surely fall.

No reports had come in from the volunteers defending those blockhouses. This indicated that the Mongols must have executed some sort of enveloping movement to isolate them before attacking—*for the purpose of keeping their new war machine secret*. It became vitally necessary to discover the nature of that machine, in order to prepare for it. And this was the mission upon which Operator 5 and Jimmy were embarked tonight. This spot was less than twenty miles from Valley Forge, and

THE COMING OF THE MONGOL HORDES

the presence of Mongols here meant that the main force under Shan Hi Mung could not be far behind. They could, by forced march, reach Valley Forge at dawn; and, if they did, with their war mechanism still a secret, Valley Forge would fall.

That was why it was necessary to let these women and children die tonight....

IN THE half minute while he watched the Mongol riflemen adjust their weapons for the slaughter of the children, Tim Donovan ran through all this in his mind, in order to convince himself that he and Jimmy were doing the right thing. Suppose they hadn't come upon this scene? Suppose they had passed a half hour later? They could not have helped. To attempt to interfere now would probably only mean the death of Operator 5 and Tim Donovan, thus leaving their mission unfulfilled. Colonel Farragut, back at Valley Forge, would be depending upon them for a report. He would expect their return. Instead, the Mongol army would fall upon him, destroy him, and march on to New York. Jimmy Christopher and Tim Donovan would have died in vain. Yet, he longed to lift his rifle and pick off those Mongols, one by one. He could feel the fierce surge of joy that welled within him at the very thought.

But, no—Operator 5 was right. They must push on. Resolutely, his whole soul crying out against it, he turned to follow Jimmy Christopher... only to find that Jimmy had halted, too, and was watching the scene below with hot eyes.

The boy thrilled. Operator 5 was wavering! He kept quiet, watching Jimmy. He could see the struggle going on within. Though he knew how important was their job tonight—how

OPERATOR 5

important that they get into the enemy lines—he hoped, with all the eagerness of his young Irish heart, that Jimmy Christopher would weaken. If there were only a way—Then a woman screamed down there, in one of the ruined buildings. It was a frightful scream, agony of bodily torture, and mental anguish over the knowledge that while she was about to be defiled, her own child would also be slaughtered outside.*

And it was the single stark scream that decided Operator 5.

"Come on, Tim!" he exclaimed. "We're going to take a hand in that party!"

---

* AUTHOR'S NOTE: To one reading an account of this period of post-invasions, it appears almost unbelievable that we should have been reduced to such a primitive existence as is here indicated. But it is a fact that there was at this time only one factory of any size on the eastern seaboard where ammunition for rifles was manufactured; and this factory was worked twenty-four hours a day to supply cartridges for American volunteers throughout the United States. Men had to be sparing of their ammunition. There were few oil wells that had not been utterly ruined by high-explosive shells, and wanton destruction, could not be operated because of lack of machinery. And nowhere along the thousands of miles of railroad track in the United States did a locomotive or electric engine function. Trains lay abandoned wherever they had run out of fuel, serving in many instances as shelters for homeless people. The great historian, Harrison Stievers, sums up the situation in a sentence when he says in Volume Eleven of his monumental work entitled, *The History of the Purple War,* "America had to be colonized over again!"

THE COMING OF THE MONGOL HORDES

CHAPTER 2
OPERATOR 5 STRIKES BACK

TIM DONOVAN'S eyes glowed. He suddenly realized that, all along, he had been certain Operator 5 would not leave without making some attempt to avert the monstrous thing about to take place in the village below.

"Okay, Jimmy," Tim breathed. "I'm with you!" He raised his rifle to his shoulder, sighting at one of the troopers who were preparing to execute the children.

There were six in the firing-squad, and one of their number—a corporal, apparently—stood to one side with saber raised, ready to signal. About fifty feet away, four other Mongols held a half dozen women at bay with bayonet points. These women were probably being kept for the pleasure of the firing-squad, after they had finished the execution of the children.

Operator 5 whispered to Tim, "You start at the right of the firing-squad. I'll start at the left."

Tim nodded, keeping his face glued to the stock of the rifle, his eye squinting through the sight. "I've got Number One lined up. Say 'when,' Jimmy!"

Tim Donovan's rifle was a Winchester high-powered automatic repeater, of which there were only a few now in use by the Americans, due to the lack of ammunition for them. Operator 5 used an old Mossman bolt-action, single-shot .22 caliber hunting rifle.

Since the destruction of the great arms factories of the country, ammunition, even for army rifles, was becoming increasingly scarce. And Operator 5 had preferred to take this antiquated, small-caliber hunting rifle rather than deprive one volunteer soldier of a good weapon. In his hands, however, the old Mossman became as deadly a gun as was Tim's Winchester.

Jimmy raised the rifle to his shoulder, said curtly, "Fire!"

Both guns spoke, simultaneously. Tim's shot slapped into the chest of the Mongol trooper on the extreme right of the firing line, while Jimmy's featherweight cartridge, directed with uncanny skill, considering the distance and the wind, caught the corporal in the temple just over the right eye.

The corporal collapsed like a deflated sack, while Tim's man was hurled violently backward by the impact of the bullet. Tim's rifle spoke again and again, as he pulled the trigger with careful, methodical accuracy, mowing down that line of executioners. Operator 5 slipped another cartridge into his arm, raised it and fired almost in one motion, his bullet catching the last man between the eyes.

So swift had been their attack, that the line of Mongol marksmen had not even had the chance to scatter. Now they were only seven still bodies lying on the ground, with a wide-eyed group of startled children staring at them from the wall.

At once bedlam seemed to break loose down there in the village. The Mongols, who had been guarding the women, ran for shelter. Others came tearing out of the cellars and shell holes where they had dragged their prospective women victims.

Tim's gun kept barking viciously, swiftly, cutting down the fleeing Mongols before they could reach cover. Operator 5, despite the fact that he had to reload after every shot, and that

THE COMING OF THE MONGOL HORDES

he had to aim with much greater accuracy to make his light-bore weapon fatal, fired almost as often, catching the Mongols as they came out of the cellars.

THE WHOLE action took place with such venomous swiftness that not more than four minutes elapsed between the first shot and the last. Yet twenty of the Mongols had been cut down. The remaining two were farther down the street, with the horses, and out of range of the two American sharpshooters on the hill. Those two, stricken with panic at the sight of their comrades being shot down, and never doubting that a powerful force of Americans was deployed in that cornfield from which death was spewing, leaped to mount their horses and escape. But now another factor entered the scene. Those women, who had seen the severed heads on the Mongol's saddles, who had been dragged into cellars while their children stood against a wall, were not to be denied. They dashed out into the street, picked up the rifles of the dead troopers, and sent a hail of lead streaming after two fleeing Mongols. The men fell, riddled with bullets. Not one of the enemy detail was left alive.

Operator 5 sighed, and lowered his rifle. "That was pure slaughter," he said.

"It's what they deserved!" Tim Donovan exclaimed. "Look what they were going to do to those women and kids!"

"Let's go down and talk to the women," Jimmy Christopher said. "We've got to get them off to safety. If this Mongol detail was so far east, it must mean that the army isn't much behind. There'll be more along soon."

The two made their way through the cornfield, down to the

village. The women saw them coming, and lined up to meet them, waving their hands, and shouting their thanks. Others knelt in silence on the ground beside the dead bodies of their old men who had been killed in the first onslaught of the Mongol detail.

The sun had dropped quite suddenly behind the western hills, and a brooding darkness was closing down.

The women clustered around Jimmy Christopher and Tim, shaking their hands, hugging and kissing them. One, the golden-haired woman whom they had seen dragged into the cellar, picked up an army coat from alongside the body of one of the Mongols, using this to cover her nakedness and protect her from the cold. She introduced herself as Mollie Blaine. Two little girls, twins of about five, with golden hair like their mother's, huddled against her while she talked to Operator 5.

"You saved my children's lives," she said. "And you saved me—from something I dare not even think of. That Mongol was a beast. He smelled as if he hadn't had a bath for a year. And his filthy hands...." She shuddered, running slender fingers over the heavy welt across her face where her captor had struck. "I'll pray for you every night, for the rest of my life," she told Jimmy warmly. "What is your name?"

Jimmy did not want to make his identity known to these people. "Captain Christopher," he said.

He didn't bother to introduce Tim. The legend of Operator 5 and Tim Donovan had spread throughout the land. The less publicity he got, the better he liked it. So he merely gave the

THE COMING OF THE MONGOL HORDES

name of Captain Christopher, hoping that these women would not see the connection.

And Mollie Blaine did not. She, as well as the other women, were too excited and grateful.

"Where is the rest of your company?" they asked him. "Why don't you bring your men out of hiding?"

"There aren't any more men," Jimmy told them with a smile.

"No more? You mean that you and the boy wiped out this whole Mongol detail between you?"

Jimmy nodded, still smiling. "It wasn't hard. We took them by surprise, and we can shoot pretty well. But now, we've got something more serious on hand. The Mongol army should be coming through here soon. You people had better arrange to get out. Start now. Use the Mongols' horses. You should be able to make Valley Forge before morning. There's a large force there, under Colonel Farragut, and they'll send you through to New York."

Mollie Blaine looked around, exchanged glances with the other women. "Are you coming back with us?"

"No," Jimmy informed her. "My young friend and I have a job to do. We're heading west."

"Toward the enemy?"

"Yes."

"B-but you're wearing American uniforms. If you're caught, they'll burn your eyes out." Her face held much concern. "We have to take that chance," Jimmy Christopher said with a smile.

HE HESITATED for a moment, looking from one eager face to the other. All were patriotic American women; many had lost husbands, brothers, fathers and sons in the two years of war. It was safe enough to confide in them, and perhaps one had noticed something that might give a clue to the secret he and Tim sought.

"We're trying to find out," he said slowly, "whether the Mongols have any special war machines that have enabled them to march from the Great Lakes without opposition. There is something—of that we're sure. And if we don't discover its nature before tomorrow morning—then our defenses at Valley Forge will fall to Shan Hi Mung's army just as ours fell in Illinois, Michigan and western Pennsylvania. That's why we're heading west tonight!"

The women exchanged glances, heads shaking. It was plain that none knew anything. Mollie Blaine was about to speak, when one of the other women uttered an exclamation of dismay, and pointed to the east.

"Look!" she exclaimed. "The Mongols are encircling us!"

Jimmy Christopher followed her pointing finger, and his lips set. What he had feared had now come to pass. On a ridge to the east, a long line of Mongol horsemen was riding, pennants streaming. It was one of the enemy columns, which, apparently, had been marching east along another road, and had now come out into the Lancaster road at a point beyond this village.

"They must be concentrating all their columns on this road," Jimmy said. "Now your retreat is cut off," he explained to the women. "You'll never be able to get through them to Valley Forge. The main column will probably appear along this road at any minute now."

THE COMING OF THE MONGOL HORDES

"What'll we do?" one of the women demanded. "If we stay here, we'll be caught by the main column. If we go back toward Valley Forge, we'll be caught by that other column—"

"I'll tell you what we'll do!" Mollie Blaine broke in fiercely. "We're going west with Captain Christopher. We'll help him look into this secret of the Mongols. He saved our lives tonight, and if he gets in a tight spot, we'll fight for him!"

"With what?" Tim Donovan asked.

Dramatically, Mollie Blaine pointed to the dead bodies of the Mongol troopers. "With their guns, and in their uniforms. We'll mount the Mongol horses, and ride west with Captain Christopher as a Mongol detail. In the dark, we'll pass, unless some of the enemy get too close to us."

"I should tell you," Jimmy Christopher said evenly, "that I don't expect to get back to the American lines alive. The way back is closed to me, as much as it is to you. But you, at least, can try to hide out in one of the abandoned mines near Coatesville. If you come with me, you're certain to be captured or killed."

"But what good will it do you to discover the Mongols' secret," Mollie Blaine demanded, "if you can't get back to the American lines with it?"

Jimmy pointed to Tim Donovan. "The boy here has a magnesium beacon flare. If we get any information, we'll semaphore it to headquarters by means of the beacon. That'll probably be the last act of our lives, because the enemy is sure to spot the beacon and come to investigate."

In the west, they could now hear the roll of enemy drums,

OPERATOR 5

THE COMING OF THE MONGOL HORDES

The next minute, like smashed flies on a table-top,
that inhuman firing squad fell in every direction.

beating out the horrible "Slaughter March" of the Mongol hordes. The main column was closing in on them.

Mollie Blaine spoke swiftly. "I think I can speak for all of us, Captain Christopher. We're going with you. We'll take as many of our girls as we have horses and uniforms for. The others will take the children and go to those abandoned mines near Coatesville that you mentioned. They'll hide there while we go with you."

Jimmy started to protest, but the women cut him short. "We can shoot," Mrs. Blaine told him, "and we can fight in a pinch. You'll need us, and you can't get rid of us!"

The women were already going about among the Mongol soldiers, stripping off their uniforms, taking their rifles and sabers. These women, brought up in the culture and amenities of American civilization before the Purple Invasion, were now doing things that they would have considered impossible two years ago. But two years of cruelty, butchery, rape and slaughter, had changed them into fighting Amazons. Within ten minutes, Jimmy Christopher and Tim Donovan found themselves in the saddle, at the head of what appeared to be a detail of Mongol troopers in somewhat battered uniforms. But strangely enough, that Mongol detail was humming the *Star Spangled Banner* as it rode westward toward the main Purple column!

THE COMING OF THE MONGOL HORDES

CHAPTER 3
WOMEN MUST FIGHT!

BETWEEN COATESVILLE and Lancaster, the road runs through comparatively level country. Though it was quite dark by this time, it was possible to see the destruction that had been wrought everywhere. Fields were overgrown with weeds, not tilled for two years. Among the charred remains of farmhouses, high mounds, alongside the road, showed where the dead had been hurriedly buried. Battles had been fought here in the early days of the Purple Invasion, when desperate American volunteers had bitterly contested every inch of ground gained by the irresistible armies of the Purple Emperor.

Here and there, they passed signs of more recent atrocities. In one small village, a dozen stark bodies hung from the gnarled, bare branches of a gaunt oak. Farther down the main street of the same village, they found the gruesome pile of decapitated bodies, whose heads still swung from the pommels of their own Mongol horses.

Those heads, in spite of the protests of the women, they had kept tied to their saddles. Jimmy Christopher had insisted that this be done. And now they were able to give those victims a decent burial, placing the severed heads tenderly and solemnly beside the bodies.

The small company lost valuable time here, digging the large common grave. But it was the least that they could do. There was no living soul near. That patrol of Mongols had denuded the town of life.

OPERATOR 5

Operator 5 said a short prayer after the first shovel of earth was laid in place, and then they started west once more. Every heart in that company was grim, every face drawn. These women had recognized many a friend, and some relatives, among the beheaded victims.

Tim Donovan patted his rifle fiercely. "Jimmy, I want to kill more of those Mongol devils!"

Operator 5 said nothing. He was thinking that all this constant, wanton butchery had cut the population of America virtually in half. Added to that destruction of life, there were the untold thousands who had died of pestilence and starvation.

The war gods were taking heavy toll of the last democracy left on the face of the earth. And now, with this Mongol scourge sweeping east from the Great Lakes, it was very doubtful if America would survive.

In Europe and Asia, the Purple Empire held absolute sway. Great arms and munitions factories were turning out cannon, bombs and planes at dizzy speed. Soon those supplies would be available to the Purple Fleet. Other armies could be brought to American shores to bolster up the Mongol legions. In Canada and South America, the Purple armies were still supreme. America was isolated, defenseless, except for the burning love of liberty which made her men fight, in spite of hardship and privation, to save their children from life under a cruel dictator.

The very flag of the Purple Empire was significant of the bloody path it had cut across the world. The insignia upon that flag was a severed head and crossed broadswords.

America's one chance was to smash these Mongol divisions

THE COMING OF THE MONGOL HORDES

of Shan Hi Mung's, before they could affect a meeting at New York with the Purple Navy and its new supplies from Europe. But unless Operator 5 could discover tonight the secret of the Mongol successes thus far, Shan Hi Mung bid fair to be in New York by tomorrow.

ABRUPTLY, JIMMY CHRISTOPHER stiffened in his saddle, and gave a low-voiced command to halt. The little column came to a stop behind him, and Tim Donovan glanced at him questioningly.

Jimmy remained silent, listening. Now, the others caught the sound—the measured tread of marching feet, low-voiced shouts, creaking of wheels. At first, those noises were only a whisper in the night from somewhere up ahead. But, as they listened, the sounds became plainer, identifiable.

And, above those sounds, there came the clatter of horse's hooves, approaching swiftly.

Jimmy Christopher called back urgently to the others, "That's the main column. There's an advance guard coming along now. We've got to take cover. Follow me!"

He pulled his horse over to one side, making for a blackened heap of ruins some two hundred feet off the road. Tim Donovan and the women spurred after him, picking their way, through stunted undergrowth, toward those ruins. The ground was hardening with the coming frost, and they had to ride carefully to keep their mounts from making too much noise.

Jimmy herded them all behind the ruins, just as the first of the advance guard came into sight. It was a strong force, almost a full company. Ahead, rode a brilliantly dressed officer, whose chain-mail glittered under the leather jacket of his uniform. He rode a huge white charger, also covered with glittering mail, and was closely accompanied by six troopers.

This small group was riding much faster than the advance guard, and, it was evident, intended to proceed ahead without waiting for the main column. Two of the troopers in the officer's escort were carrying flaring torches which illuminated the road ahead, enabling them to gallop at a swift pace. Operator 5's eyes narrowed as he noted that a third trooper was carrying a long pennant from which flew—not the severed head and crossed broadswords of the Purple Empire, but a white flag of truce!

Tim Donovan exclaimed, "Look, Jimmy! They're sending someone ahead with a flag of truce. You think they want to make peace?"

Operator 5 laughed bitterly. "Peace! Of course—on their terms! They've done that before every important battle. They demand unconditional surrender, as the price of sparing the lives of our women and children. Some day, they'll get tired of sending that same demand all the time!"

Mollie Blaine, who was peering out from behind the ruins beside Jimmy, whispered, "I know that officer. We saw him in the village last year, when the Mongol divisions were quartered on us. It's Captain Lord Wai-tan, the nephew of General Shan Hi Mung. He's even more cruel than his uncle. He delights in butchering and torturing prisoners with his own hands!"

"Captain Wai-tan, eh?" Jimmy Christopher said reflectively. "I've heard of him, all right, but I've never seen him before. I'd like to meet him in battle some day!"

THE COMING OF THE MONGOL HORDES

JIMMY CHRISTOPHER

OPERATOR 5

CAPTAIN WAI-TAN and his escort disappeared down the road, and the advance guard, carrying flares of their own, drew abreast of the ruins where Jimmy Christopher and his group were hiding.

Operator 5 whispered to Tim, "See that the women are careful not to let their horses make a sound." Then he turned to watch the road. The advance guard was proceeding more slowly now, and Jimmy feared that they might send out scouts on either flank. In that event, they would surely discover his presence here. And, if they *were* found, their Purple uniforms would do them no good. At this range, they certainly could not hope to be mistaken for Mongols.

But the commander of the advance guard did not send out scouts. Apparently he was secure in the belief that there were no American fighting forces between here and Valley Forge. Also, the Mongols no doubt were depending on their numerous scouting patrols, like the detail that Jimmy and Tim had ambushed.

The advance guard passed on down the road, with their flares, and a short period of complete darkness ensued, during which Jimmy Christopher caught the sounds of the rhythmic tramping of many thousands of feet coming along from the west.

"That's the Mongol infantry," he told Tim Donovan. "And, listen—" he tautened, gripped the boy's shoulder with a hard hand—"do you hear that creaking noise again—like the sound of huge wagon wheels? That's what I want to see—the thing that's making that noise!"

They waited patiently in the darkness. Operator 5 was

THE COMING OF THE MONGOL HORDES

conscious of the responsibility of those women, behind him. He had tried to discourage them from coming along with him, but the more dangerous he had painted the undertaking, the harder they had insisted. He scarcely dared to hope that he would be fortunate enough to discover the Mongols' war secret as easily as this. That creaking sound might have nothing at all to do with it.

But if it should, by chance, reveal the thing he wanted to discover, then he and Tim would have to act swiftly and risk everything in a desperate attempt to communicate their knowledge to Colonel Farragut at Valley Forge. And Operator 5 was afraid that Mollie Blaine and her friends would prove more of a hindrance than a help.

But he shrugged that thought aside, and watched the road keenly. He could hear the women whispering in the shadow of the ruins in back of him, and the stirring of the horses. Now and then, he caught a faint *click* as one of the women cocked her rifle in preparation for instant action, should that become necessary.

He frowned, and called back to them, "There's to be no fighting. If we're discovered, we mount and ride for it. If we learn anything here, and if Tim or I should be killed or wounded, you are not to wait for us, but try to make your way back to the American lines with the information."

Now the vanguard of the Mongol host came into sight. A solitary drummer led the way, followed on horseback by an officer. Close behind the officer came two ensigns, bearing flags. One was the flag of the Purple Empire, with its grisly severed head and crossed broadswords; the other was the standard of Shan Hi Mung, the Mongol war lord. This one

OPERATOR 5

was hardly less terrifying, for it bore a replica of an ancient Chinese ceremonial dragon, spouting fire from its nostrils, and with its immense torso coiled in a crushing grip about the waist of a naked woman whose breast was pierced with a glittering spear. That dragon flag of the Mongols had waved over many an atrocity. Now it was marching to the  measured, deliberate beat of that drum in the vanguard, heading toward the sack of New York.

Behind the ensigns appeared the marching column of Mongol infantry, ten abreast, in measured tread. They filled the road, these fierce and lustful warriors of a barbarous war lord, and the flares carried by the torchbearers at the side of the road threw an eerie, ominous gleam upon their blood-encrusted bayonets, and the gleaming mail of their armor.

The torchbearers were captive Americans, marching with shackles on their legs, half-naked and shivering in the bitter cold of this December night. They were compelled to hold their torches high aloft, as they marched, and, if one weakened and lowered his torch for a moment, an ever-watchful guard thrust the tip of a bayonet into the unfortunate man's back, to spur him on. If he stumbled and fell, unable to go farther, the guard would run him through the stomach, and leave him there to die slowly, in untold agony, on the frost-bitten road.

Tim Donovan, standing beside Operator 5, gritted his teeth audibly. "God, Jimmy, I can't stand looking at that!"

THE COMING OF THE MONGOL HORDES

"Steady, boy!" Operator 5 put a hard hand on his shoulder. THE LAD subsided, and they silently watched the mighty Mongol divisions march on. That creaking noise, which Jimmy had heard before, grew louder. Now, they could hear cries of anguish mingling with the creaking—cries punctuated by the sharp, cruel crack of whips upon human flesh, and high-pitched oaths in the language of the Mongols. Jimmy Christopher and Tim Donovan, with the women behind them, stared in tense amazement at that which now came into view.

It was a tall wooden tower on wheels, rising perhaps sixty feet from the ground, and constructed of huge timbers rough-hewn from giant oak and pine trees. At the top of the tower, a tremendous length of virgin timber protruded upward at an angle of about seventy degrees toward the rear. The lower end of this log rested upon an axle running athwart the tower. The upper end was scooped out into the shape of an immense spoon. A complicated series of pulleys and twisted ropes crisscrossed between the spoon-shaped timber and the tower itself. Halfway up the tower, another great log protruded toward the front, its end sharpened to a tip which was capped by dark, burnished metal.

On the roof of the tower, some two dozen Mongol troopers were resting.

But the thing that attracted and held Operator 5's attention—and the attention of every one of his small group hiding there behind the ruins—was the means by which this huge, unwieldy tower was being transported. Its huge cartwheels creaked as the tower moved. *And it was drawn by a long quadruple line of American captives, yoked to it like so many oxen!*

OPERATOR 5

At either side of the long line of human dray animals, guards marched with long, snapping horse-whips. Those whips cracked through the air, descending upon the backs of the American captives, driving them faster.

For a long moment, Operator 5 was silent, gazing upon that weird engine of war, illuminated as it was in ghastly fashion by the dozens of torches carried alongside it. Then he swung swiftly to Tim Donovan.

"Tim! That's the answer! That's why the Mongols have broken down our defenses. Tim, we've got it!"

The boy was puzzled. "What is this fool thing, Jimmy? Why do they make our poor boys drag it around?"

"Don't you see, Tim? They've taken a page from ancient history. In the olden days, before there were firearms and cannon, they had to use these things to demolish enemy forts. And they're using it now, too. That thing is a *ballista*—a catapult. See that big timber at the top? They put a rock in the spoon of it, and pull it way down by pulleys. Then, when they release it, those twisted ropes unwind like a flash, and the lever jumps up, hurling the projectile with irresistible force. It could smash through the wall of one of our puny blockhouses as if it were cardboard."

Tim Donovan gazed at the *ballista*, wide-eyed. "Gosh, Jimmy! No wonder they smashed our defenses!"

"And that other log in the middle of the tower," Jimmy Christopher went on, "is a battering-ram, operated on the same principle as the catapult lever. They pull it way in, then let it go. It'll smash down a wall."

THE COMING OF THE MONGOL HORDES

"But what'll we do, Jimmy? How can we build a fort strong enough to resist it?"

"We'll have to stop building blockhouses. We'll have to concentrate on trenches, only. The catapult isn't much use against a trench, except to drop some rocks here and there. But it wouldn't do the same damage."

Jimmy Christopher turned to the women. "You've all seen that." He motioned toward the creaking catapult in the road. "It isn't the only *ballista* tower the Mongols have." He pointed into the night, up the road, where the flares of hundreds of torches illuminated the tall outlines of dozens of other similar towers, coming up behind the first.

"It's our job now to get word of this to the American lines. We're going to try to get out of here now, to some hilltop where Tim can use his magnesium beacon flare to semaphore a message to Colonel Farragut at Valley Forge. If, for any reason, we are prevented from semaphoring, each of you must attempt to win her back to our lines with this information, as I told you before. That is your duty. If we're discovered, it'll be every one for himself—or herself. We'll separate, because individuals would stand a better chance of getting through than a large company like ours. Is everything clear?"

Mollie Blaine and the other women chorused acquiescence.

Jimmy nodded. "All right. Mount your horses. We'll try to get away now."

OPERATOR 5

CHAPTER 4
SIGNAL OF DEATH

THEY WERE about to obey, when Mollie Blaine suddenly pushed forward alongside Operator 5. She pressed close beside him, looking toward the road, where the second catapult tower had come abreast of them, drawn by its quota of captives. Mollie Blaine uttered a deep sigh that was almost a groan, and Jimmy could feel her body shivering beside him.

"Gerald!" she exclaimed in a low, agonized voice.

Jimmy saw that her eyes, suddenly filmed with tears, were fixed upon the captives who were serving as human oxen for the second catapult.

"Gerald!" she repeated again. When she turned to Operator 5, her lips were twitching with emotion. "It's—my husband! There—in the first row. See him—with the torn shirt!"

Operator 5 followed her pointing finger, and he spied the man she meant. Mollie Blaine's husband! There he was, the first one in the left-hand row of captives. There was a crude bandage about his head. The yoke about his shoulders seemed to weigh down his stocky frame. He was laboring to keep up his end of it. Each of those captives tried to do as much as he could, so that his fellow prisoners would not be shouldered with his portion of the labor. But it was easy to see that Gerald Blaine was almost at the end of his rope.

As they watched, a guard raised his cruel horse-whip, and

THE COMING OF THE MONGOL HORDES

brought it down in a stinging blow upon Blaine's shoulders. He winced, but did not cry out, stumbled on.

Mollie Blaine uttered a choked cry, and made as if to run out into the road. Operator 5 threw an arm about her waist, dragged her back. She struggled for a moment, then subsided, gasping.

The other women crowded about her, soothing her. She raised great pain-racked eyes to Operator 5. "Can't we do anything for him? He's my husband. I—I can't stand by and—see him suffer like that!"

Jimmy regarded her compassionately. "That's the whole Mongol army out there," he said. "What can the twenty of us do against them? If we should throw away our lives in a useless attempt to rescue Gerald, the Americans at Valley Forge will all perish. Also, there will be thousands of other captives to take their places beside your husband. Do you think he'd want it that way?"

Mollie Blaine lowered her eyes. "N-no. He went to join the volunteer force at Chicago, and was captured. I—I haven't heard from him for three months. It—it was a shock to—see him like that. But you're right, Captain Christopher. We—we can't do anything."

Jimmy hesitated, thinking. Then he suddenly appeared to make a decision. "I'll tell you what, Mollie Blaine. If we succeed in getting our message to Valley Forge by semaphore, and if these other friends of yours are willing, I'll help you try to rescue him!"

The other women instantly approved the proposal. Mollie Blaine stared at Jimmy almost unbelievingly. Then a glad, wistful smile lit up her face. "If you do that," she said, "I'll be your slave for the rest of my life!" Before he could stop her, she snatched up his hand, raised it to her lips.

He drew it away, motioned for them to mount. "Let's go!" he said almost gruffly.

IN A moment, the small company was on its way, working south across a barren field, away from the enemy column, and toward a hill which Jimmy had spotted about a half mile away. "If we can make that hill," he told Tim Donovan, "we can set up the magnesium beacon. I think we can get our message to Farragut—he's watching for it. But between you and me, Tim, I don't think we'll leave that hill alive. The lighting of the beacon will bring the Mongols down on us like a swarm of hornets."

Tim nodded gravely, looking wise beyond his years. "It's pretty tough to think about dying, Jimmy. I've followed you through some bad spots in the past, and we've come out of them. But I think you're right about this time. We're asking for it."

He paused a moment. "You know, Jimmy, it's not so hard to think of dying, when there is so much killing going on all around. You sort of get used to it."

Jimmy Christopher reached across and pressed the boy's hand, on his pommel. "Good kid, Tim. If we go, we'll go out fighting, anyway. I'm sorry about these women, though."

"And Diane will be sorry, too. Gosh, Jimmy, I hate to think of her when she gets the news that you've finally cashed in."

They rode in silence after that, each thinking his own thoughts; Operator 5 made the pace, and was careful that it should not be too fast, lest they attract undue attention. They

THE COMING OF THE MONGOL HORDES

had already been seen by the troops in the road, for they were forced to show themselves in crossing the field.

But there were other Mongol patrols scouting the woods and fields now, spreading out fanwise from the main column, and their uniforms in the night lulled any possible suspicion.

Now they were at the foot of the hill, and Jimmy urged his mount up the narrow path to the top. There was another patrol not a hundred feet away, and he was anxious to get to the top before they should hail him. Though he spoke the language of the Purple Empire fluently, he was not as adept in the outlandish tongue of these barbarian Mongols, and would betray himself should he attempt to answer.

The women crowded their horses close behind him and Tim, and they luckily reached the top of the hill without being hailed. There had once been an old farmhouse here, but it had been razed to the ground, only charred timbers remaining.

Jimmy used his night glasses. He had a good view of the country for miles in either direction. Far to the west, he could see a great red haze in the sky. He knew that this must come from the town of Lancaster, which the Mongol troops were passing through. The barbarians were no doubt burning the city to the ground.

To the west, he could see in the distance, a multitude of flickering torches. That would be Valley Forge, where Colonel Farragut was laboring with his volunteers to build a blockhouse and a series of breastworks—defenses which those huge catapults in the road would crumble to pieces!

TIM DONOVAN had already dismounted, and was busily

OPERATOR 5

engaged in setting up the magnesium beacon, which he had carried strapped to his back like a knapsack. He worked with it a few moments, and a bright red flare sprang up from it. The flame rose to a great height, and would be visible for miles around—to the Mongols as well as to Farragut's men at Valley Forge.

"All right, Jimmy," Tim called to him. "I'm ready. What's the message? I'll send it in Morse code. Diane'll be with Farragut, and she'll be able to decipher it."

Jimmy Christopher nodded. He had trained Tim Donovan as well as Diane Elliot, his sweetheart, to send and receive Morse Code. Now, that training was to come in handy.

"Send as follows," he dictated. *"Abandon building of blockhouse...."*

As he spoke, Tim stood over the magnesium beacon with a large, cup-shaped lid. He raised and lowered this lid, cutting off and opening the flame in a series of dots and dashes. He was sending the message. The danger was that the Mongols might also be able to read Morse. In any event, the very fact that they were signaling from here would inform the Mongols that they were enemies. Everything depended upon how quick-thinking they were—whether there would be time for Tim to send the entire message.

"Tim Donovan reporting," he clicked off in Morse. *"Abandon building of blockhouse.... Mongols have cat...."*

And that was as far as he got. The Mongols had, indeed, thought fast. For a detachment of riders had swung out from the road, and were racing across the field, rifles barking. Behind them, another detachment fell in, and charged across the field.

THE COMING OF THE MONGOL HORDES

Tim began the semaphore message, hurriedly.

Up the path of the hill, they came, rifles blazing. Some officer there in the line of march had recognized the danger of the semaphore, and he would certainly receive a great reward from Shan Hi Mung tonight for his quick action.

OPERATOR 5

And now the Mongols were on the top of the hill, riding full tilt at the small group of women who had formed a line alongside Operator 5. Jimmy Christopher called out to them, "Remember what I said. Don't fight! Retreat down the other side of the hill. Every one for herself—and try to get through to our lines!"

The women hesitated for a moment, and Jimmy shouted at them savagely, "Get out!"

His tone spurred them. Mollie Blaine led them, as they swung their mounts around, and raced for the road down the other side of the hill.

Operator 5 backed his horse up alongside Tim Donovan. "It's the end, Tim!" he shouted. "Keep that semaphore going!"

He reached out and pulled Tim's repeating-rifle out of the saddlebags of the boy's horse, and coolly began to fire into the throng of cavalry charging at them. He shot slowly, methodically, each shot telling. The Mongols were so many that their very numbers made them clumsy. They bunched in the trail, and Jimmy Christopher fired twice, hitting the two leading horses, sending them back on their haunches to crash into those behind. The Mongols were thrown into confusion, milling wildly around. Their advance, for a moment, slowed up.

Jimmy Christopher turned around for a quick glance at Tim. "How are you doing—"

He broke off, the words choking in his throat.

Tim Donovan lay slumped over his semaphore. The beacon had gone out, because, as he fell, Tim's metal cup must have

THE COMING OF THE MONGOL HORDES

covered the flame, putting it out. The message had not gone to Farragut!

"Tim!" Jimmy Christopher bent low over his horse's side. His anguished glance told him that the boy's scalp had been grazed by a bullet. He was unconscious, but not badly wounded.

Now, the Mongols in the path began to fire once more, and Jimmy saw that they had formed their ranks anew, were about to charge down upon him.

He reached down far over the side, gripped Tim's collar. He heaved up, exerting almost superhuman strength, and raised the boy, swung him over his pommel. Then he dug spurs into his horse, and raced away, the Mongols less than fifty feet behind.

The darkness helped, but also hindered him. Though it kept the Mongols from shooting accurately, it also prevented Operator 5 from making real speed. He had to pick his way down the steep road, and the Mongols were gaining.

He passed a great rock in the side of the road, and bullets from the enemy rifles were screeching close to him. He could not hope to escape—they were too close.

But, suddenly, unexpected assistance appeared. From behind that rock, a veritable hail of lead poured into the Mongol pursuers. Their leading men and horses were cut down, hurled back into the others, throwing the whole company into terrible confusion.

Jimmy Christopher looked up toward that rock, and smiled. Mollie Blaine and the women hadn't run. They had waited here to see if they could help!

While the Mongols were still in wild confusion, the women

poured round after round into their ranks, until they turned and ran, leaving their dead and wounded behind.

Now, Mollie Blaine and her Amazons came out from the shelter of the rock.

Jimmy Christopher waved to them. "Thanks!" he called. "This way!"

He led the way down that back road, with Tim Donovan, unconscious, in front of him. They had been close to death that time, but once again, it had passed them by. The boy would recover. Operator 5 wondered whether there was anything to the theory that only those who are not afraid to die deserve to live.

Mollie Blaine spurred her horse alongside him. "The boy?" she asked anxiously, glancing at Tim Donovan's inert form.

"He's only stunned," Jimmy told her. "He'll come out of it soon. When we get a chance, I'll patch his scalp. We'll have to look sharp from here on, Mollie Blaine. They'll be after us in hordes. We couldn't get the semaphore message through. That means we have to make the American lines before the enemy gets to Valley Forge. It also means that we have to give up the idea of rescuing your husband."

She replied, very low, "All right. I know who you are now. You're Operator 5. We'll follow you—to hell, if necessary."

CHAPTER 5
ULTIMATUM FROM THE DEVIL

THE MOON, bright with a hard, brilliant light, seemed to be grinning down with ironic grimness upon the

THE COMING OF THE MONGOL HORDES

devastated field of war-torn America. The water of the historic Schuylkill River reflected a murky, sulky iridescence in the night, its rippling waves flickering under the lights of a hundred torches.

Held aloft, they were like so many giant fireflies, moving fitfully in the hands of their bearers, who stood there, hour after hour, faithfully.

By the aid of the illumination furnished by those torches, four companies of Farragut's Fifth American Engineers were laboring, in a desperate race against time, upon the erection of a blockhouse.

This was Valley Forge, on the bank of the Schuylkill River, where, once before in our nation's history, a bedraggled, hungry, ill-clad army had wintered under the command of General Washington. And now, as then, America was fighting with her back to the wall.

On a knoll overlooking the Schuylkill, a small group of officers, and one young woman, stood in earnest conference while the engineers labored upon the blockhouse.

The commanding officer, Colonel Farragut, was gazing worriedly through a night telescope toward the west. Far in the distance, a great glaze reddened the sky, rising apparently from some immense conflagration. Colonel Farragut muttered, "Looks like there's a fire somewhere around Lancaster. Say, there's a signal beacon burning!"

He focused his glass upon a flare, which appeared much nearer than the big blaze. This smaller flare was being doused intermit-

OPERATOR 5

tently, in short and long flashes, like the dots and dashes of Morse Code....

Farragut motioned to an officer in the small group. "Get out the code book, Brown. That's a message!"

Before Brown could comply, the young woman who stood at Farragut's elbow said quietly, "If you'll give me the glass, Colonel, I can read that message without the aid of the code book."

Farragut stared at her a moment. "All right, Miss Elliot. Here you are!"

The girl, who was scarcely more than twenty-two or three, took the glass and focused it upon the beacon. Diane Elliot was dressed in ragged, torn riding-breeches, a lumber-jacket over a denim blouse. Her auburn hair was disarranged, but she did not seem to mind. In spite of her bedraggled appearance, and the weariness that shone in her face, her soft beauty was apparent to every one of those officers.

Her lips moved swiftly, spelling out the letters that were flashing fitfully from that beacon far out in the night. As she read the letters, Farragut swiftly wrote them at her dictation upon a pad.

The message, as she spelled it out to Farragut, read as follows—

> Tim Donovan reporting. By order of Operator 5. Abandon building of blockhouse. Mongols have cat—

Suddenly, Diane Elliot uttered an exclamation of dismay. Her

THE COMING OF THE MONGOL HORDES

slim body tensed. "The beacon—it's gone out! They've broken off the message!"

A grim silence spread among the small group of officers. For a moment, no one spoke. All stared anxiously toward the west where that beacon had shone only a moment ago.

At last, Colonel Farragut said stiffly, "They must have been surprised by a Mongol advance guard. I warned Operator 5 not to go out on that scouting party himself. We need him too much to risk him that way."

One of the other officers said hopefully, "Perhaps they weren't captured. Perhaps they were just scared off by the Mongols."

Diane Elliot shook her head. "I know Operator 5—and Tim Donovan. If they had even only a moment, Tim would have flashed us a signing-off signal."

Colonel Farragut turned heavily away from her. He said bitterly: "Operator 5 has always been too reckless. Now, whatever may have happened to him out there, he leaves us with a terrible problem." He turned to watch the engineers working on the blockhouse. "We have barely five thousand men here. And we're supposed to stop the advance of an army of two hundred and fifty thousand Mongols!"

"Not stop them," Diane Elliot corrected him. "Only to hold up their advance until New York can finish its preparations for defense. If New York should fall to the Mongols, there'd be nothing left of America."

Farragut nodded. "You're right, Miss Elliot. We'll hold Valley Forge, all right—while there's still a man left alive among us!"

OPERATOR 5

His voice dropped an octave. "Just the same, I wish Operator 5 were here to shoulder the responsibility."

HIS EYES swept the scene of activity about them. The blockhouse was being erected on the rising ground near where they were standing, less than two hundred feet from the river. This was the second highest point in the Valley Forge section. It was the spot where McIntosh's Brigade had been encamped when Washington's army wintered here. Farther to the south and the west, two long lines of trenches were being dug, running parallel with the Valley Creek Road, and converging on Mount Joy.

The logs for the blockhouse, and the sandbags for the fort, were being hauled in by American volunteers, who had yoked themselves to the long wagons, like oxen.*

---

* Author's Note: Those readers who have studied the history of the Purple Invasion will, of course, be familiar with the events of the preceding two years. Those who wish to refresh their recollection—namely, the capture of the Purple Emperor by General Shan Hi Mung—are referred to the preceding issue of this periodical, containing the novel entitled, "The Bloody Frontiers."

The whole story of the Purple Invasion has, of course, become an epic of American history. At the time when the Purple Emperor was only the dictator of a single militaristic European nation, none in the United States dreamed that his mailed fist would one day be placed upon our throats. We were an industrial, peace-loving nation in those days. But we carried our love of peace too far. We failed to appropriate sufficient moneys for the modernization of our army and navy and air force. Thus, when the Purple Emperor had made himself master of Europe and Asia by conquest, and sent his

THE COMING OF THE MONGOL HORDES

Farragut was busily issuing orders for the hurried completion of the blockhouse, and Diane Elliot was left to herself now for a moment. She stood there quietly, while the men labored all about her, and her thoughts flew to the westward, where that beacon had appeared. She knew that Operator 5 and Tim Donovan were out there in the night, perhaps already prisoners of the Mongols, or else hard-pressed by those merciless warriors of the Mongolian war lord.

Her hand clenched upon the revolver strapped at her slender waist. If there were only something she could do to help them! She turned to see Colonel Farragut approaching her once more.

The colonel gave her a sympathetic glance. "You're worried about Operator 5?" he asked.

She nodded. "He and Tim Donovan must have been caught by surprise," she told him. "I have half a mind to go and see what

combined armies to our shores, we were unable to offer effectual resistance to his huge tanks, his super-dreadnoughts, his highly mechanized infantry with their long-range artillery.

It was only through heroic sacrifice, under the leadership of that man, who was known in the American Intelligence only as "Operator 5," that we were able to break Emperor Rudolph's grip upon the country. But his vast armies were still at large, threatening in many distant parts at the same time. Though our own navy had been utterly destroyed, the huge Purple Fleet was still on the waters, with enough ammunition to shatter every one of our coast cities. Weakened and disheartened by two years of warfare, the American morale was well-nigh broken by this new threat from the Northwest.

OPERATOR 5

DIANE

COL. FARRAGUT

CAPT. WAI-TAN

THE COMING OF THE MONGOL HORDES

MOLLY BLAINE

GEN. SHAN-HI-MUNG

TIM DONOVAN

happened. They couldn't have been more than five miles away. If you could give me a fresh horse—"

Farragut shook his head. "I won't let you do it, Miss Elliot. It's too dangerous. You know what those Mongols are doing to their prisoners? They burn their eyes out with hot irons. That's only one of their little tricks. No, you'll stay right here. I've thrown out additional patrols on all the roads. If Operator 5 and the boy are making their way here, pursued by the enemy, the patrols should contact them. That's the best I can do for them. As for you, I order you to remain here."

Diane Elliot lowered her eyes. She recognized Colonel Farragut's logic, but every fiber of her rebelled against remaining inactive here while Operator 5 was in danger. She was about to speak once more, when a shrill whistle sounded from the direction of the outer breastworks, down near the Valley Road.

Farragut frowned. "That's one of the outpost sentries, signaling for the officer of the day. Something's turned up."

Diane's eyes lit up. "Maybe it's Operator 5!"

The colonel shook his head. "Impossible. He couldn't have got here so quickly. But—"

He broke off as the sound of drumming hooves came to them. Someone was spurring up the hill. In a moment, an orderly appeared, riding fast. He flung himself from the horse, and saluted.

"Lieutenant Calhoun's respects, sir. There is a Mongol officer at the outer lines, with a flag of truce. He wishes to talk with our commanding officer."

The colonel nodded. "Bring him in. Blindfold him."

THE COMING OF THE MONGOL HORDES

The orderly saluted and left. Diane waited impatiently. Farragut led her to one of the tents which were being used for headquarters until the blockhouse should be completed. "We'll talk to him in here," he said. "The less this Mongol sees of our activity now, the better I'll like it."

The tent was a large one, with a table at which Farragut seated himself. He motioned to Diane to take one of the chairs. "You might as well sit in on this," he said.

Diane nodded her thanks, but did not sit down. She could not get her mind off Operator 5 and Tim Donovan. Many times in the past, when danger had threatened one or the other of the small group of Operator 5's assistants, she had had the same feeling that affected her now. More than once, the life of one or the other of them had been saved by the impulsive action of some member of the group. And she wanted to ride west now, to look for them.

HER THOUGHTS were interrupted by the arrival of the Mongol officer. He was escorted into the tent by Lieutenant Calhoun, the officer of the day. Calhoun saluted the colonel. "This is Captain Lord Wai-tan sir, the nephew and personal adjutant of General Shan Hi Mung. He comes under a flag of truce. He was accompanied by an escort of five Mongol troopers. They are waiting for him at the outer lines."

Farragut nodded. "You may remove your blindfold, Captain Wai-tan."

The Mongol raised a hand to his eyes, and pulled off the bandage. He was a short, stocky man, in his early thirties. His high cheekbones glistened in the light of the candle on the colonel's table. His small eyes darted around the interior of the tent, and fastened upon Diane Elliot.

Diane met his glance, and a sudden feeling of revulsion went through her. It was as if some inner prescience were warning her that this Mongol captain was going to affect her life enormously. She saw his lips part, revealing sharp pointed teeth beneath the shaggy, overhanging moustache. He wore some sort of glistening chain-mail beneath his leather jacket, and his queer helmet sat low on his forehead. A jewel-studded sword hung at his side. But the thing that disgusted Diane more than anything else was the fact that there were flecks of dried blood on his jacket, and on the tall boots that he wore.

Colonel Farragut said, "You have a message, Captain Wai-tan?" His voice was dry, uncompromising. He, too, had seen those spots of dried blood, and he knew what they meant. This officer had no doubt partaken in the massacres which had taken place in every town and village on the route of the Mongol march from the. Northwest. Harrowing tales had filtered through of the heartless cruelty of Shan Hi Mung's troops. This man looked the merciless butcher that he must be.

But Colonel Farragut kept his temper, remembering that the fellow was here under a flag of truce, and that as long as he had been received under that flag, his person was inviolate.

The Mongol captain answered Farragut's question, but kept his eyes continually upon Diane. He spoke a fair brand of English, as did most of the officers of the Purple armies, for they had lived among Americans for almost two years now.

"I come as the emissary of my exalted uncle, Shan Hi Mung,

THE COMING OF THE MONGOL HORDES

the general of all the Mongols, and the most loyal servant of His Imperial Majesty, Rudolph I, Emperor of the Purple Empire!"

He rolled the words with all the overbearing insolence which these conquering vandals had developed in the two years during which they had ridden rough-shod over a bleeding America.

Young Lieutenant Calhoun, standing just within the tent, grew red in the face, and took an involuntary step forward, but stopped at a glance from Farragut. The colonel frowned. Wai-tan's eyes were still fixed upon Diane. They were traveling over the rounded slimness of her slender body with a lasciviousness that he did not bother to hide.

Colonel Farragut said sharply, "Why do you keep up the pretense of representing Emperor Rudolph? Everybody knows that he is the prisoner of Shan Hi Mung!"

Captain Wai-tan shrugged. "General Shan Hi Mung marches east in the name of the emperor," he insisted. "I bring an ultimatum from him!"

"An ultimatum?"

"You must evacuate this position at once, and leave the way clear for our armies to march to New York. If you do that, then the lives of your women and children will be spared. Otherwise, all will die in every town that falls to us!"

He smiled thinly, watching Diane all the while that he spoke.

Colonel Farragut half-rose from his chair, and his lips clamped together. "Is that what you came here to tell us—under the protection of a flag of truce?"

"That, and more. You do not realize the weakness of your position. General Shan Hi Mung has two hundred and fifty

OPERATOR 5

thousand men. If you refuse to accept our terms, we will strike with all our strength, here—tomorrow morning. How can you hope to resist? We know that you have only five thousand men. How long can five thousand stand against odds of fifty to one?"

Farragut lowered his eyes. "You seem to be well informed."

Wai-tan grinned thinly, his cruel lips twisting under the mustache. "War is our business. We know everything that we have to know. We know that your troops are spread all over the country, that you cannot afford to concentrate a great number of men at any one point, because the disbanded Purple soldiers are raiding everywhere. But my master, the Lord Shan Hi Mung, has the greatest army of all the Purple generals. And the Purple navy, under Admiral von der Selz, is cooperating with us. When we have driven you out of this position, and are ready to march upon New York, von der Selz will sail up the Hudson River with his fleet, to take the city in the flank. New York must fall to us."

Wai-tan leaned forward, for the first time taking his eyes from Diane and fixing them upon Farragut. His voice dropped to a threatening purr. "You will save your people much pain and agony if you will surrender. It will be terrible for them, if you should make us fight to capture New York!"

Farragut's face clouded with anger, and he arose. "You can go back to your war lord, Captain Wai-tan. You can tell him that he is going to have to fight for every inch of ground that he takes. Now get out—before I forget that you are here under a flag of truce!"

Wai-tan was about to make some insolent reply, but he caught the gleam in Farragut's eye, and perhaps thought better of it. He

THE COMING OF THE MONGOL HORDES

shrugged. "As you say, Colonel." He backed out of the tent, and Lieutenant Calhoun tied the blindfold around his head once more. The young lieutenant smiled, nodded toward Farragut. His lips formed the words, "Good work, Colonel!"

Calhoun took the Mongol captain by the arm, led him out into the night.

COLONEL FARRAGUT seated himself again, and his fingers drummed nervously on the table. He looked at Diane Elliot. "You know, Miss Elliot, everything that Mongol butcher said was true. We can't hope to resist them. If only Operator 5 were here!" His head shook.

Diane Elliot moved toward the entrance. "Of course, it's out of the question for us to give up. We've got to fight. And maybe something will turn up."

"Where are you going?" Farragut asked her.

Diane's face assumed an expression of innocence. "Oh, just to wash up—and look around."

She hurried from the tent, and Farragut looked after her with a puzzled glance. But he shrugged, and turned to the papers on his table, ringing for an orderly. He might have been much more concerned had he seen what Diane was really doing.

Once outside, she walked quickly among the laboring Americans, following in the wake of Lieutenant Calhoun and the Mongol captain. She followed them through the encampment, to the outer lines, and watched while Wai-tan's blindfold was removed, he mounted his horse and rode away into the night with his squad.

Then she ducked behind a rifle-pit to avoid being seen by

55

OPERATOR 5

Calhoun as he made his way back toward headquarters. Once the lieutenant was out of sight, she hurried out from concealment, ran swiftly across to the compound where the horses were kept. The guard at the stockade gate knew her, and greeted her in friendly fashion.

"Quick!" she breathed. "Get me a horse!"

He looked at her doubtfully. "Have you got a pass from the colonel?"

"There's no time for a pass," she told him. "I've got to follow that Mongol squad."

The guard complied with her request reluctantly. He knew that she had the run of the encampment, and that she was here more or less as a free-lance, taking orders only from Operator 5. He brought her a horse, saddled and equipped with rifle and canteen. "It's dangerous out there, Miss Elliot," he warned her. "Two of our patrols haven't come back."

"Don't worry," she called back, over the drumming of her horse's hooves, as she cantered away.

She headed out into the night, along the Lancaster road, which Captain Wai-tan and his escort had taken. Her face was set, her lips tight. She was going to follow through to no-man's land behind the Mongol squad—to look for Operator 5 and Tim Donovan....

THE COMING OF THE MONGOL HORDES

CHAPTER 6
THE MAN WHO GAVE AWAY AMERICA

GENERAL SHAN HI MUNG, warlord of all the Mongol divisions of the Purple Empire, smiled, and twirled his mustache. He reached over and moved a bishop three squares diagonally along the red. "Check!" he said.

His opponent, seated across the gilt-and-lacquer-covered table, frowned, glaring down at the chess board.

Shan Hi Mung's cold eyes glittered. "You see, my dear Emperor, it is checkmate, as well. Your king has no alternative. He has lost all his support, while I remain with two bishops, a queen, a knight and a rook."

The man whom Shan Hi Mung addressed as emperor made an impatient gesture, and swept all the pieces from the board in a petulant fit.

"Must you beat me every game, Shan Hi Mung? Can't you leave me some little pride? After all, I am your emperor—even though I am your prisoner, as well!"

Shan Hi Mung spread his hands deprecatingly. "Let us say you are my guest, sire. I only keep you with me for your own protection. When my armies are victorious, I shall see that you are once more recognized as the Emperor of the Purple Empire. Until then, I want to be sure that your navy will cooperate with me, and that the war supplies coming from your European factories will be delivered to me. Believe me, Emperor Rudolph, I do not wish to take your place as emperor of the world."

OPERATOR 5

Shan Hi Mung leaned forward over the table, and his bright eyes locked with Rudolph's. "But I want America! I want to be the master of America. You can have the rest of the world. I've served you well, Rudolph. My armies helped you to conquer Europe and Asia. My armies helped you to conquer America."

Rudolph I broke in with a harsh, bitter laugh. "To conquer America!" he snorted derisively. "What sort of conquest is it, when we have had to fight a beaten people? These Americans are mad, I tell you. They do not know when they are beaten. I had the country at my feet, from coast to coast. Then they rose up, without weapons, and *broke* my empire! Had it not been for the stubborn resistance of this mad people, led by that super-mad Operator 5, I would still be emperor of the world, and not your prisoner!" Veins of anger showed in the emperor's forehead. His words came with a hissing venom that was terrible to behold.

"I hate them—the Americans. I want to see every one of them die in agony... especially Operator 5."

Shan Hi Mung's thin smile still persisted. "I will catch him for you, sire, I will give him to you. But you must give me America!"

Rudolph did not meet the Mongol general's glance. The huge caravan wagon in which they were riding with the Mongol army was furnished with an extravagant splendor that exceeded the wildest imagination.

The caravan, itself, was fashioned exclusively of inlaid teakwood, shipped all the way from the East. Priceless hangings, filched from American museums, covered the walls. The furni-

THE COMING OF THE MONGOL HORDES

ture was a collection of antiques taken from American national monuments.

The wagon was divided into two rooms—one in which these two sat, and another, separated by hangings behind Shan Hi Mung's chair. The other room was the bedroom. The whole affair was drawn by forty American captives, yoked into the traces. It was in this fashion that General Shan Hi Mung led his army to battle. They were proceeding eastward on the Lancaster Road, toward Valley Forge. Couriers and officers were constantly entering and leaving the moving vehicle. A brick fireplace had been built into one corner of this room, and it was glowing redly now, heating the whole wagon.

At the elbows of the two men, there were golden goblets, in which rested an amber liquid, thick sweet wine from Turkestan. Servants stood behind the chair of Shan Hi Mung, as well as of Rudolph, prepared to execute their every wish. This sumptuous caravan wagon was the last word in luxury, rivaling the traveling equipment of any eastern potentate in the old days of greatness.

Emperor Rudolph's small, shrewd eyes studied the Mongol general. "If you will give me the live body of Operator 5, Shan Hi Mung, I will forgive this imprisonment, and I will let you have America for yourself."

"You must hate him very much then, sire."

Rudolph did not reply. Only his eyes glowed an unholy red in the reflection of the candlelight.

Shan Hi Mung smiled, and raised his glass. "Let us drink to the speedy capture of Operator 5—and to my installation as

OPERATOR 5

Emperor of America. On that day, you shall be free to depart for Europe, sire."

Grudgingly, Rudolph raised his own glass, and they sipped the fragrant wine.

The wagon passed over a rough spot in the road, and jolted a little, spilling some of the wine from Shan Hi Mung's glass. He frowned, but continued to drink.

THE CURTAINS behind the Mongol general parted, and a woman appeared from the bedroom beyond. She was tall and sinuous, and her body was white and soft, contrasting strikingly with the utter blackness of her hair and eyes. She wore a sort of night-dress, consisting of silken, diaphanous pantaloons, and a silken sleeveless jacket which open at the front exposing the soft rounded smoothness of her breasts. Her mouth was a hot, curving, sensuous splotch of red, capable of being utterly cruel; and her dark eyes shone like jet out of her high-cheeked, Eurasian countenance.

She stood there, half-smiling, conscious of her beauty, enjoying the frankly admiring gaze of Rudolph. Shan Hi Mung, seeing the direction of Rudolph's glance, turned in his chair. His eyes glowed with a fierce possessiveness.

"Mistra!" he exclaimed. "You are more beautiful than ever. I thought you were sleeping."

She pouted. "I was asleep. But those clumsy Americans jolted the wagon, and awoke me."

THE COMING OF THE MONGOL HORDES

Shan Hi Mung smiled cruelly. "They shall be punished." He raised a hand, and an orderly stepped forward from his position near the door.

"Have the carriage halted. Take ten of those American swine out of the traces and spit them on bayonets, as an example to the others. Let them be more careful in the future!"

The orderly saluted without expression, and climbed out. In a moment, the carriage stopped. Mistra smiled slowly, voluptuously. She moved to a chair beside the table, seated herself, and a servant poured her a goblet of wine. She sipped the liquor languidly, while the eyes of Shan Hi Mung devoured the beauty of her body.

After a moment, there came quick cries of anguish from outside in the road, followed by groans of agony. Shan Hi Mung put a hand on her knee. "They are punished," he said.

Mistra arose, went to a window and peered out. She laughed throatily. "The soldiers have left those Americans with the bayonets still in them, at the side of the road. It is very funny, how they wriggle!"

The orderly returned, and bowed low from the waist. "The master's orders are fulfilled. Ten other Americans have been yoked up to replace those punished. We are ready to proceed, master."

Shan Hi Mung was about to give the order, when another orderly appeared, and saluted. "Master, the Captain Lord Wai-tan has returned from the American lines. He has a prisoner."

"Send him in."

OPERATOR 5

Shan Hi Mung glanced at Rudolph. "The Americans have, of course, refused to surrender. I am interested in this prisoner that Wai-tan thinks important enough to bring to me."

In a moment, the Captain Lord Wai-tan entered leading his prisoner by a halter around her neck.

The captive was Diane Elliot.

Her hands were tied behind her back. Her blouse was torn down the front, revealing the glowing vitality of her body, in sharp contrast to the soft, white, voluptuous beauty of the dark-haired Mistra. The halter about her white throat was pulled tight, so that the least jerk of the rope dug the noose into her skin. She faced Shan Hi Mung and Rudolph unafraid, her lips drawn tightly together, and her eyes sparkling defiance.

Mistra's face clouded as she saw Diane Elliot's wholesome beauty, and she threw a quick, troubled glance in the direction of Shan Hi Mung. She said nothing, but her lips curled in a half snarl, and her hand stole to a jeweled dagger sheathed at the waistband of her silken pantaloons.

CAPTAIN WAI-TAN bowed low with a triumphant smile. "Revered uncle," he said, addressing the Mongol general, "my mission to the Americans was devoid of success. They are stubborn. They refuse to surrender. But—" he cast a proud glance at Diane—"I had rare good luck afterward. As we were returning here, we heard a horse's hooves pounding behind us. We spread out in ambush and captured this girl. My lord, I saw her in the tent of the American colonel, Farragut, and I recognized her there. She is—"

THE COMING OF THE MONGOL HORDES

He was interrupted by the eager voice of Emperor Rudolph. "She is the Elliot girl—Operator 5's sweetheart!"

Shan Hi Mung's obelisk eyes glittered. "This is rare good fortune!" he said softly. He studied Diane, and she felt naked under his scrutiny. "Why were you riding toward our column in the night?" he asked her. "Were you expecting to meet someone—Operator 5, for instance?"

Diane looked at him defiantly. She did not answer.

Wai-tan laughed shortly. "She is obstinate, venerable uncle. I have already tried to make her talk."

"She must talk!" the general exclaimed. "She must have had an appointment to meet Operator 5—else, why would she be traveling into enemy territory alone? And if Operator 5 is somewhere inside our lines, I want to know. As I said—" he glanced significantly at Rudolph—"it would be great good fortune if we could catch that man... so soon after our little compact."

Rudolph leaned forward eagerly. He wet his lips with his tongue. "Make her talk, Shan Hi Mung."

The Mongol general nodded. He drew from his belt a long, wicked bone-handled knife with a blade that was a thin sliver of flexible steel. He handed this to a servant. "Heat the blade in the fire," he ordered. "Heat it till it is white-hot!"

Captain Wai-tan shifted uncomfortably from one foot to the other. His ugly, square face expressed a number of mingled emotions. "Revered uncle," he said diffidently, addressing Shan Hi Mung, "I have a favor to beg of you. This woman—I saw her in the tent of the American colonel, and she was very beautiful,

OPERATOR 5

and I wanted her for myself. I beg of you, revered uncle, do not disfigure her, for then she will not be beautiful any more."

Shan Hi Mung gazed at his nephew amusedly. "You want this woman of Operator 5's? Tsh, tsh. There are many others."

"No, my reverend uncle. It is this one that I want. I beg of you."

Shan Hi Mung frowned. He watched Diane, saw the revulsion in her face. They had been talking in the language of the Purple Empire, for the benefit of Rudolph, and Diane understood. Shan Hi Mung saw her shrink almost instinctively from the gross figure of Wai-tan.

The servant brought him the white-hot knife, and he fingered it meditatively. "We must compel her to talk, Wai-tan. An empire is in the balance for me. But—" he smiled cruelly—"I am inclined to think that there is another way to make her talk. Take her, Wai-tan. Take her into Mistra's bedroom, here. See if you can induce her to talk. If you succeed, then we need not disfigure her—and you can have her. But if you fail, then we will have to—use my little toy here." He waved the blade.

Wai-tan was overjoyed. He seized Diane by the shoulder. "Come."

"Wait!" Shan Hi Mung rose. He frowned disapprovingly at his nephew. "When you take a woman like this, you do not want to bring her to the bridal couch with bound hands. Let me free her." He swung Diane around roughly, so that her bound wrists were before him. Then he placed the white-hot blade of his knife between them, and cut through the cords. The hot steel sizzled against her wrists, and the odor of scorched flesh filled the room.

THE COMING OF THE MONGOL HORDES

Diane shuddered, bit her lip to keep back a groan, and raised her chin. Her eyes watered at the agony of her seared wrists, and she raised them, shaking off the ends of the cord.

Red welts appeared on her hands where the knife had touched them.

Shan Hi Mung laughed cruelly. "That is how I free you," he said. "Be careful that I do not attempt really to hurt you. Do not anger me by refusing to talk."

He motioned to Wai-tan. "Take her, my nephew. I give you an hour to drag the information from her. After that, *I* will try with her."

Wai-tan licked his thick lips. "After an hour, reverend uncle, I will give her back to you!"

He put a heavy hand on Diane's bare shoulder, started to drag her toward the other room.

THE WOMAN, Mistra, was watching avidly, enjoying the way things were turning out. She had feared, at first, that Shan Hi Mung, himself, might take a liking to this virile American girl. Rudolph's small, beady eyes were fixed upon Diane, as Wai-tan dragged her out. He was drinking in every bit of it, storing it up, so that on the day that he had Operator 5 in his power, he could relate to him all the details of what had happened to his sweetheart… and watch him squirm.

But Diane Elliot had been thinking fast. There were, in that room, an orderly and three servants, besides Wai-tan, Shan Hi Mung, Emperor Rudolph, and the woman, Mistra. The door was guarded, and she could not hope to escape that way. Even

OPERATOR 5

if she did, she would be in the midst of the Mongol army. She saw her one chance, and she took it.

She allowed Wai-tan to drag her halfway into the next room. She offered no violent resistance, but just as Wai-tan started to follow her through the hangings, she whipped up her scorched hand, and snatched the sword out of the scabbard at his side.

The blade came out with a long *swishing* sound, and Wai-tan uttered an ejaculation of surprise which was cut short, as Diane threw off his grip upon her shoulder, and swung the blade up so that the point was touching his throat.

"If you move, I'll kill you!" she told him.

Wai-tan was too startled to move. But Shan Hi Mung sprang from his chair, while the orderly at the door drew a revolver from his belt.

Diane reached out and gripped the front of Wai-tan's uniform, at the same time keeping the point of the blade at his throat. She called out urgently to the Mongol general, "If anyone in that room takes a step nearer, Shan Hi Mung, I'll run this blade through your nephew's throat!"

Shan Hi Mung stopped, and motioned to the orderly to put the gun back. His eyes blazed at the nephew's back, and he uttered a string of expletives in some Mongolian tongue, that made Wai-tan's ears grow red. But he dared not move, dared not try to shake loose from Diane's grip upon his coat, lest she thrust the sword home.

Diane backed slowly into the bedroom, drawing Wai-tan after her.

Other men might have doubted that so beautiful, so cultured

THE COMING OF THE MONGOL HORDES

a girl could bring herself to thrust that sword into a man's throat. But these Mongols were so used to daily cruelty, that they took it as a matter of course. Even at that moment, ten captives were twisting in agony out on the roadside, with bayonets in their bodies. Shan Hi Mung was certain that his nephew would die instantly, if a move was made toward him.

Wai-tan, himself, looking into Diane's eyes, less than three feet from his own, knew also that she would not hesitate to kill him, because he read there the cold courage that lay behind them. He heard many stories of her exploits, both alone and in the company of Operator 5. From those stories, he knew that she possessed the courage to kill.

Besides, there was every reason, as far as he could see, why she should drive that sword home into his throat to protect herself. His own creed of ruthlessness dictated it. Had he not intended to submit her to indignity and shame—and then turn her over to be tortured? He was her enemy—and, under the Mongol creed, one's enemy must be crushed utterly.

His small, desperate eyes never left hers. He did not cease to desire her because of this exhibition of her courage. Rather, he wanted her the more... wanted to humble this high spirit....

THE ONLY one in that elaborate carriage who was not certain of how she would act if rushed—was Diane herself. Diane had fought side by side with American troops, battled her way out of tight spots at the side of Operator 5. She had often escaped by killing soldiers on the field. She could shoot almost as well as Operator 5, and far better than most other men. But this was different.

OPERATOR 5

Diane swung the blade so that it pointed squarely at Wai-tan's throat!

The American nature does not turn readily to the use of cold steel. In addition, she had never killed a defenseless person in cold blood. This was as near to cold blood, as possible. For Wai-tan was entirely at her mercy. Even as she held the point of the weapon at his throat, she wondered if she would really

THE COMING OF THE MONGOL HORDES

drive it home should Shan Hi Mung and the others in the room disregard her threat.

But she bluffed boldly. Her voice held no single trace of weakness, as she issued her ultimatum. Slowly, firmly, she dragged Wai-tan into the bedroom. The hangings closed behind them, shutting them off from sight of the others. She backed Wai-tan into a corner, and pulled over a chair, seated herself. She lowered the point so that it rested in the groove where his chain-mail shirt met the tops of his leather boots. She sat so that she could see the door, as well as keep him covered. "Stand very still. If anyone steps through those hangings, I'll run the sword into your stomach."

He smiled twistedly. "How long can you remain like this? You will grow tired, perhaps sleepy—"

"You had better hope that I don't," she told him, trying to sound cold and heartless. "Because, the moment I begin to feel tired, I'll finish you off. If they get me, Mr. Wai-tan, you, at least, will go with me!"

He believed her, and paled a little.

In the next room, Diane could hear them moving about, whispering among themselves. She did not know exactly what she hoped to accomplish by this bold move. Only, she knew that she was at least delaying the cruel torture that Shan Hi Mung kept in store for her. Something might turn up....

In the other room, Shan Hi Mung was standing in uncertainty, eying the hangings. A slight smile was upon his lips. "What a woman that is," he muttered. "I would like to tame that little spitfire." He turned to the others, spread his hands. "What shall we do?" he asked. "I must find some means of saving my nephew."

The dark-haired Mistra glided up to him. "Let her stay there," she murmured. "She will grow tired, and we will rush her."

Emperor Rudolph broke in, "I have an idea, Shan Hi Mung!"

He arose from his chair, and came around beside the Mongol

THE COMING OF THE MONGOL HORDES

general. His eyes were glittering. "Let us send word to the Americans that we hold the Elliot girl a prisoner."

Shan Hi Mung frowned. "To what purpose?"

Rudolph smiled knowingly. "I have had occasion to learn the nature and temperament of this Operator 5. When he learns that the Elliot girl is here, he will risk everything to save her. It has happened so before, only he was clever enough to trick us. This time, though, we shall be ready for him. We will set a trap for him. He will surely come, and we will snare him."

Rudolph paused, and Shan Hi Mung's features broke into a cunning smile. "That, sire," he said softly, "is a stroke of genius. We shall do it that way!"

Mistra's eyes were dreamy. "I should like to meet this Operator 5," she said speculatively. "He inspires such hate in you both, and he defies you so successfully—such a man must be interesting!"

They glared, outraged by her insinuations. She dropped her eyes.

CHAPTER 7
VENGEANCE RIDES HARD

SOME TWO hours before dawn, a Mongol patrol might have been seen, riding swiftly along a side road leading north, just outside of Coatesville.

Dozens of similar patrols were out now, scouting in every direction, for the Mongol army of Shan Hi Mung was approaching Coatesville, and the vanguard was due to enter the town within twenty minutes. This was so close to Valley Forge that the Purple troops would be deploying into battle formation upon passing through Coatesville.

Most of the other scouting parties were sending back messengers at intervals, to report the condition of the roads, and the layout of the surrounding terrain. But this particular detail sent no messengers back. In fact, it was trying to avoid other Mongol troops as much as possible.

At the head of the small column, Operator 5 and Tim Donovan urged their weary horses forward unremittingly, while Mollie Blaine and her twenty women companions followed close upon the heels of the leaders.

Mollie Blaine spurred ahead of the other women, pushing up alongside of Jimmy Christopher. "Slow up here," she directed. "The Straley Coal Mines should be around the next bend. That's where I told the women and children to hide."

Operator 5 nodded, and slowed down to an easy canter. "We'll have to work fast," he said. "How many of the women and children were there?"

"About eighteen," Mollie informed him. "We'll have to double up with them. It'll slow us up, and we haven't got much of a lead on the Mongol army, anyway."

"It can't be helped," Jimmy said. "If we leave them here, they're sure to be found by the Mongol scouts. I'm going to ask two of you to ride ahead, and warn Colonel Farragut of the Mongol catapults. The rest of us will follow, with the double load."

He was about to take the bend in the road, when he abruptly pulled up his horse, motioning to those behind him for quiet.

THE COMING OF THE MONGOL HORDES

He glanced significantly at Tim Donovan. "Did you hear that?" he asked in a whisper.

Tim shook his head, but listened. And then he caught the sound that Operator 5 had already detected. It was no one single sound, but rather a multitude of noises, each in itself almost indistinguishable, but blending together in the night to give the little group here a picture of what was going on around the bend in the road. There was the shuffling of iron-shod hooves on gravel, the slap of leather harness, the occasional clink of metal, mingled with low-voiced commands.

Mollie Blaine, who had pushed up close to Jimmy, exclaimed, "It's a troop of cavalry! They must have found the women and children hiding in the mine!"

Jimmy nodded grimly. He dismounted swiftly, motioning for the others to remain up in the saddle. Then he stole forward quietly until he reached a tree just at the bend of the road. He crouched, peering around the bole of the tree. What he saw caused his lips to tighten, involuntarily. The road here debouched into an open clearing facing the low slope upon which the coal mines were located. At the top of the slope was the tipple house, resting on stilts, and from the tipple house a long chute ran down the side of the slope toward the railroad tracks which crossed the road.

In the clearing, half a hundred Mongol cavalry were gathered, sitting their horses at ease, while two officers stared up at the mine buildings. It was apparent that the Mongols had in some way discovered that the women and children were in hiding up there in the mine, and were figuring the best means of capturing them!

JIMMY CHRISTOPHER, watching behind the tree, was conscious of Tim Donovan and Mollie Blaine, crawling up to join him. Mollie peered over his shoulder, and choked back a gasp at sight of the clearing full of enemy soldiers. "There must be fifty of them!" she exclaimed. "Too many for us. And we can't do anything to save the women and children. My own two little girls are up there—"

Jimmy raised a hand to silence her. The two officers were turning back to the troop. Moonlight glinted upon the epaulets of one of them, revealing a silver numeral, X. This indicated that the man was a centurion captain, commander of a company of a hundred men in the Mongol army.

"We should be thankful that he only has half his company here," Jimmy whispered to Tim Donovan and Mollie Blaine.

Mollie gripped his sleeve. "Those women up there don't know that the Mongols are down here. Can't we fire off a gun or something, to warn them? They could escape down the other side of the slope."

Jimmy shook his head. "They'd never get away. This road runs around the slope, out in back of the mine. The Mongols could ride around, and catch them coming down."

"Then—there's no chance?"

"Wait. Let's see what they intend to do."

The two officers mounted their horses again, and rode across the clearing, talking together. They were quite close to where Jimmy and the others were crouching now, and it was possible

THE COMING OF THE MONGOL HORDES

to hear what they were saying. They were talking in the Mongolian tongue, and though Jimmy Christopher was no expert at it, he yet knew enough to get the gist of what the captain was telling his lieutenant.

"You will take half of the company, Khalum, and ride around to the other side of the mine. I will give you four minutes to place yourselves. Then I will have the bugles sounded, and flares lit. Those women will see us down here, and will try to escape the other way. That will be your chance to seize them. Do not cut them all down. Save them for the camp-fire. We will have rare sport with them to divert the men before we attack the American position at Valley Forge in the morning."

The two officers rode among the troopers, and Mollie Blaine plucked at Jimmy Christopher's sleeve, whispering in voice fraught with muted agony, "They're going to torture them all night. My two little girls—and all my friends, and their children!"

The other women crowded around Mollie Blaine, who told them what was happening.

Jimmy could see that panic was rapidly seizing them at the thought that they would have to witness the capture without being able to help. Jimmy was thinking fast, concentrating upon the problem. The danger was real, and imminent. There were twenty-two of them—one man, one boy, and twenty women—against a thoroughly armed, vicious company of fifty Mongolian cavalrymen. But the enemy was dividing now, and that might make the odds more even. Suddenly, his eyes flashed with inspiration, and he called to them urgently.

OPERATOR 5

They gathered around him, and he explained his plan: "While those troops are riding around the side of the slope, I'm going to try to steal across the clearing, and up the front of the slope—if I can get to the tipple house without being seen. I want you all to remain here with Tim Donovan. Dismount, and spread out on both sides of the clearing. When these men here light their flares, open fire on them. Keep shooting as fast as you can. Fire by relays, so that you can keep up a continuous barrage. That'll make the  enemy think there's a large force attacking them. Meanwhile, I'll try to get those women and children down this side into the clearing, while the other half of the enemy is still looking for them on the *other* side. Is that clear?"

The women nodded bewilderedly, and Mollie Blaine began repeating the instructions. Jimmy motioned her aside, impatiently. He glanced at Tim Donovan, who nodded his head to indicate he understood Jimmy's plan.

Operator 5 said, "Take your orders from Tim. He knows what to do!"

He squeezed Tim's hand, and moved away from them, cutting through the woods at an angle so as to come out into the clearing as close to the railroad tracks as possible. Behind, he could hear the Irish lad giving terse, low-voiced instructions.

THE COMING OF THE MONGOL HORDES

HE REACHED the edge of the clearing, and peered out. The enemy company was already divided into two sections, and the lieutenant was leading his command along the road, skirting the slope of the coal mine. The other half, under command of the captain, was grouped closely together, listening to his instructions.

Jimmy Christopher got down on all fours, and crawled out into the open. He took out his revolver, and kept it in his right hand as he crept toward the railroad tracks. If he were spotted, his Mongol uniform would not save him—and he did not intend to be captured alive.

There were some thirty feet across the clearing, between him and the railroad tracks. Beyond the tracks, the ground sloped sharply upward to the mine building, or tipple house, which was at the top of the shaft. It was up there that the coal was sorted, then sent down the covered chute into waiting freight cars on the tracks.

Now, of course, the tipple house and the chute were not in use. The mine had been abandoned many months before, when a purple shell had caved in the shaft. Another shell had struck a couple of freight cars down at the mouth of the chute, demolishing them, and also demolishing the shed into which the chute conveyed the coal before dumping it into the cars.

Jimmy Christopher figured that if he could reach the shelter of those wrecked freight cars, he would be safe, for he could then climb the slope in the shadow of the chute. But the ticklish part of the job was the task of getting across that clearing. The moon was throwing a dull silvery glow across the cleared space, and

OPERATOR 5

the Mongol horsemen were curbing their restive animals not twenty feet from where Jimmy crawled. If one of them should look in his direction, he was lost.

But their captain was speaking to them in the short, close-clipped, high-pitched accents of the Mongol tongue, and they were paying him close attention.

Lieutenant Khalum and his detail had already disappeared around the side of the slope, and the Mongol captain was ordering several of his men to spread out, with flares ready to light. There was only another two minutes grace during which Jimmy Christopher could hope to make the railroad tracks undetected. He got to his feet, and ran, bent low. The distance toward the tracks decreased—twenty feet, fifteen, ten; he was almost there. And the captain's voice rang out in a sharp order.

"Light the flares!"

Matches rasped in the night. Flame spilled from the flares. Jimmy threw himself headlong to the ground, under the shadow of the demolished freight cars, just as the fitful blaze of those torches illuminated the clearing. He wriggled across the tracks, hugged the wooden structure of the coal chute, and began to run uphill. He was out of sight of the Mongols in the clearing below, but he could see the glowing reflection of their flares. And abruptly, several rifle shots split the silence of the night. They were shooting to scare the women and children up there in the mine—and startle them into running.

Jimmy lengthened his stride, reached the top. The long, low shed of the tipple house stretched at his left. Down below, the shouting and the shooting increased in intensity.

THE COMING OF THE MONGOL HORDES

Jimmy ran along the side of the tipple house, seeking a door. He found it, and heard frantic voices within. The door pushed open, and a frightened group of the women, carrying their children in their arms, streamed out, heading toward the rear of the slope. They were doing just what the Mongol captain had predicted they would—running down the back, directly into the arms of Lieutenant Khalum and his men.

Jimmy Christopher hurled himself among them, desperately. "Wait! Wait !" he shouted. "Not that way! They've set a trap for you!"

The women leaped back from him in terror, seeing only the hated Mongol uniform. But the moonlight shone on his face for an instant, and they recognized him as the man who had saved them from the Mongol detail. They crowded about him, asking hopelessly what they should do.

"Inside!" Jimmy ordered.

HE LED them back into the tipple house. Within, the shed was pretty much in the condition in which the Straley Company had abandoned it. Rows of bins, now empty of coal, lined the walls. At the far end were the conveyor belts which had been used to carry the coal up from the mine shafts; and across from those belts was the chute down which the coal had been sent to flow into the freight cars on the tracks below.

The women and children crowded, frightened, around Jimmy Christopher, as he threw a hurried glance about the room. He ran to a window, peered down into the clearing. He smiled bleakly. Tim Donovan and Mollie Blaine and the others had carried out his orders. He could see flashes of rifle-fire darting

OPERATOR 5

from a dozen points in the woods surrounding the clearing, and he could also see Mongol cavalrymen falling from their horses. They had been taken utterly by surprise.

Jimmy ran to the rear window, and frowned. It appeared that Lieutenant Khalum had not been satisfied to wait patiently down below for the refugees to run into his trap. He was leading his detail on foot, up the back of the slope, toward the tipple house!

Those men of Khalum's would reach the top of the slope before Jimmy could possibly hope to shepherd these refugees down to the clearing. They would be able to pick them off at their leisure, or capture them without trouble.

The women had their arms around the little tots now, and had herded them into a corner. All were resigned to their fate. They'd been through so much of recent months, that they were used to the imminence of death. Their eyes followed Jimmy's swift movements as he hurried around the huge chamber, inspecting it, seeking desperately for some means of escape. He cast another glance down toward the clearing, and saw that the last of the Mongol horsemen were spurring in flight around the bend in the road, which would take them out behind the mine. The clearing was in the hands of Tim Donovan and Mollie Blaine's women. But how to get his own refugees down there, without exposing them to the fire of Khalum's detail?

Operator 5 stood there in the middle of the tipple house, his forehead creased in frown, every nerve taut.

The hoarse shouts of the Mongols came to them, as Khalum's men dashed up the slope toward the door. Suddenly, a flash of

THE COMING OF THE MONGOL HORDES

inspiration lit up Jimmy Christopher's countenance. He called to two of the women, handed one his revolver, the other his rifle.

"Get behind one of those bins," he commanded, "and cover the doorway. Shoot every time you see a Mongol face!"

The women took the weapons, looking at him bewilderedly. They certainly would have wanted to shoot it out with the enemy, rather than be captured without a fight; but they couldn't understand why he gave them the guns instead of fighting, himself.

Nevertheless, they took up the positions he indicated to them, and watched the door, throwing an occasional eye at Operator 5. At first, they could not understand his queer actions. For he climbed up on to the platform which led to the chute, and peered down into it, throwing the beam of his flashlight along its dark interior. Then he got down from the platform and went over to the windows, peered out into the clearing below. They were in almost complete darkness here, except for three small candles, which were guttering to an end, and for Operator 5's flashlight.

NOW, FROM outside, came the heavy tread of feet, and the guttural voice of the Mongol lieutenant, issuing orders.

Jimmy Christopher called out, urgently, "Put out all the candles. Watch that doorway. Everybody but the two girls I gave the guns to—come over this way. Feel your way carefully!"

He was back on the platform again, and, as the women and children put out the candles and moved toward him in the darkness, they suddenly understood his plan. A low cheer went up from among them. He was going to slide them down through the chute to the safety of the clearing below!

The Mongol troopers outside were lighting flares, and several

OPERATOR 5

of them must have got hold of a log which they used as a ram, for there now came shattering impacts upon the door. The door did not give, but Jimmy could hear the creak of the flimsy timbers. It would not last long.

In the dark, the breathing of the women and children could be heard distinctly.

Jimmy Christopher gave his low-voiced commands. "Now then, who's first? All right, lady, take the baby in your arms. Climb in here. Hang onto my neck. The chute is a little rough, but you'll have to bear it. There's a sandpile at the bottom, and you'll fall easy. All right, let go!"

There was a gasp, and a sliding sound, and the first of the refugees was on the way down through the covered chute.

The Mongols were battering hard at the door. They couldn't get at the windows, for the ground sloped away from the door of the tipple house, leaving the windows some ten or twelve feet above their heads. Jimmy went on calmly with the work of sending the women and children down the chute, waiting just long enough between passengers to give the previous one time to reach the bottom.

He counted them as he helped them onto the platform in the darkness, and, when he had dispatched sixteen, he breathed a sigh of relief. That would leave only the two women he had stationed to watch the door.

The battering-ram was having its effect, and the door threatened to go any minute. Jimmy called out, "All right, you can leave your posts, girls. You're next."

The two women backed up to the platform, and handed him

THE COMING OF THE MONGOL HORDES

the guns again. He put the rifle down, and helped them, one after the other, into the chute. Just as the second went sliding down, the door gave with a loud crash, and fell inward. The Mongol troopers crowded in, trampling over it, raising the torches high above their heads to illuminate the entire room.

Jimmy Christopher raised his revolver, fired six times in quick succession, smashing his slugs into the Mongols in the doorway. He staggered them back upon those behind, crowding the narrow passageway, littering it with dead and wounded.

The thunderous reverberations of his quick shots echoed through the room, as he put a leg over the side of the chute, prepared to pick up the rifle and slide, before the Mongols could recover from their confusion. In the glare of the torches outside, he could see the vindictive countenance of Lieutenant Khalum, pushing through the doorway over the bodies of his men.

Jimmy reached down, put his hand on the rifle, and then vaulted over onto the chute. Then there came a crumbling roar below him.

He held on, not letting himself slide, and felt the chute tremble beneath him. It was collapsing!

The chute had probably rotted through lack of use, and now the weight of the women and children had weakened it. Less than ten feet from the roof, the chute caved in, blocking off his escape.

Outside, Lieutenant Khalum uttered a wild shout of triumph, and leaped into the room. Half a dozen troopers followed him. They raised their rifles to fire, and Jimmy vaulted from the chute,

OPERATOR 5

dropping face down on the platform just as a blast from their guns screamed past over his head.

HE LAY at full length on the platform, firing quickly but accurately. He picked off three of the Mongol troopers who had leaped ahead of the lieutenant, and then the others ran for safety to the protection of the wooden bins that lined the walls. From the protection of these bins, they opened a concentrated fire upon Operator 5, sending a continuous hail of slugs beating against the sides of the platform. Luckily, the platform was considerably higher than the floor—the only thing that kept Jimmy from being literally swept off it by that drumming barrage.

The troopers in the bins were aided by their fellows still outside, who began to fire at Jimmy from the doorway. These troopers were so infuriated by the fact that one man was defying them, that they concentrated all attention upon him. They knew, of course, that the refugees had escaped down the chute into the clearing below, but they were apparently unaware of the fact that their captain and his men had been attacked and routed. Therefore, they assumed that the refugees could not go far, but would be easily captured at the bottom of the chute.

They kept firing from three sides, and Jimmy Christopher replied only when they attempted to rush him. The lieutenant, from the protection of one of the bins, ordered a rush. Six men spread out fan-wise, advancing toward the platform under cover of the barrage.

Jimmy fired coolly, sighting by guesswork rather than vision, for he dared not raise his head. The end must come soon now.

THE COMING OF THE MONGOL HORDES

Still, he managed to pick off two of the troopers who rushed him, and the others leaped for cover once more. The lieutenant, kneeling behind his bin, was pulling the pin from a grenade. Jimmy had jerked his head up for an instant, and glimpsed that action. Then a slug whined past his ear, and he dropped flat again. In another five seconds, if the lieutenant's aim was good, that grenade would land on the platform, and explode, sending him into eternity.

Jimmy's lips tightened. He squirmed forward, toward the edge of the platform, risking a bullet between the eyes. The lieutenant had half risen from behind the bin wall, his arm high in the air to hurl the grenade. Instantly, Jimmy Christopher snapped a shot at him. The slug smashed the lieutenant's wrist.

The grenade jerked from the man's hand, fell out into the aisle between the bins, and rolled for a few feet. The Mongol troopers uttered shouts of terror, and started to stream out from the bins, seeking to escape from that deadly bomb. But they were too late.

The grenade exploded with a blinding flash. The concussion shook the whole building. The walls trembled, as if an earthquake were shaking them. Jimmy Christopher was almost hurled from the platform, though he was a good twenty yards from the explosion. But he gripped a stanchion, held on grimly. On the floor below him, mangled bits of flesh and uniform filled the air, and hissing flames licked up from the bins. The building had caught fire, and the mangled bodies of the lieutenant and his men lay in the heart of those flames.

The men who were still on the outside uttered cries of rage. They began to fire at the platform once more, in the attempt to keep Jimmy Christopher inside that flaming building. But, abruptly, the crackling of other rifle-fire sounded from farther down the slope, and those Mongols began to melt away from the doorway.

Jimmy smiled tightly. Tim Donovan and the women had not failed him. They had come up to his aid! He leaped from the platform, ran toward the door. The flames had not yet spread to this end of the building, and his path was clear. He got outside in time to see the last of the Mongols fleeing down the slope, while Tim Donovan and the women picked them off. There was no mercy in these women for the Mongols who had maimed and tortured their children. They kept shooting until the last Mongol fell.

TIM DONOVAN came running over, panting. "Gosh, Jimmy, it's good to see you all in one piece. We were afraid you might have been caught in that fire!" He gazed at the blazing tipple house.

Jimmy Christopher said, "We better get out of here. Those flames will attract every Mongol patrol in the neighborhood. Are the women and children safe down there in the clearing?"

Tim nodded. "They all came down fine. We won't have to mount double on the horses. We've captured about thirty extra mounts from the Mongols!"

They moved away from the burning building, which had served as a crematory for the Mongol troopers and their lieutenant. Operator 5 led the way soberly down the slope.

Death might still overtake this little company of refugees before they reached the American lines. It would soon be dawn,

THE COMING OF THE MONGOL HORDES

and they were still more than an hour's ride from Valley Forge. Far too much time had been spent here, and they dared not use the Lancaster road, for the Mongol main column must be very close. They would have to make their way to Valley Forge by back roads, and yet get there quickly enough to warn Colonel Farragut of the catapult towers.

Jimmy Christopher, for the first time, felt weary. If America could only purchase a month of peace—a month of respite from this bloody business of war—no price would be too dear. No price? He laughed grimly to himself, and Tim Donovan threw him an anxious glance. Yes, there was a price which America would *not* pay—the price of the lives and happiness of its women and children.

Diane Elliot—the thought of her quickened his pulse. He had not seen her for several days. He wondered, knowing her impulsive nature, whether she had been content to remain quietly in Valley Forge while he was away on this expedition. Somehow something—a faint prescience of evil that he could not define—tugged at him.

Had he known that at that very moment Diane Elliot was sitting in the bedroom of a Mongol carriage caravan, holding a sword to a man's waist, it is questionable which way he would have ridden that night. As it was, he saw that all the refugees were mounted, then set out, leading them by back roads, toward Valley Forge and temporary safety.

Mollie Blaine spurred up alongside him. Her two children were safe now, riding in the arms of women in the column. But Mollie was pale, distraught, nervous in the darkness. "You—you won't forget your promise?" she asked Jimmy. "You promised to try to rescue Gerald."

"I won't forget," he told her. He could sympathize with this brave woman, whose husband, half naked, back scarred by a cruel lash, was yoked to a huge war machine of the enemy. Jimmy had promised to try to save him, and meant to carry out that promise.

He did not know how closely linked that promise was to the fate of the girl he, himself, loved….

CHAPTER 8
TO DIE AT DAWN

THE ALARM was out. Along the length and breadth of the Mongol column, couriers were hurrying, semaphores flashing. Word was spreading to every Purple detachment on the march to Valley Forge to be on the lookout for the band of American raiders who had wiped out a half company of Mongol cavalry at the Straley Mines. Operator 5 halted his weary group in a small thicket less than a hundred yards from the Lancaster Road. Ahead, they could see clearly the fitful scurrying lights of the American engineers at the Valley Forge encampment. Behind them, less than a half mile away, the Mongol army was deploying into battle formation. Bugles were blowing. The tall skeletons of the catapult towers were visible, moving slowly forward within range. Mongol skirmish lines were spreading out fanwise toward the first line of the American redoubts.

A troop of Purple infantry was moving up the road toward the thicket that concealed Jimmy Christopher's party.

THE COMING OF THE MONGOL HORDES

Tim Donovan leaned sideways over his horse, and nudged him. "We can't stay here, Jimmy. The Mongols will spread out, and we'll be cut off. We had better ride in—"

"Wait!" Operator 5 silenced him, raising field-glasses to his eyes. He studied a semaphore beacon that was flaring a message, about a mile to the west, from the heart of the Mongol column. "Take this down, Tim—quick!"

He watched the dot-and-dash message, reading it fluently to Tim, who wrote down the letters as he dictated. At the end of the message, Jimmy Christopher's throat was dry, his lips set grimly. Mollie Blaine and the women sat their mounts quietly behind him, while he took the pad upon which Tim had written the Mongol words. His eyes blazed as he read them over—

> All patrols and skirmish parties are instructed to watch for American raiding party believed to be headed by Operator 5. They are disguised as Purple cavalry. Inform all units that the girl, Diane Elliot, is our prisoner. She dies one hour after dawn, and all Americans at Valley Forge will see the spectacle.

Tim Donovan said, almost in a whisper, "It—it can't be true, Jimmy. It can't—"

Operator 5 smiled wryly. "It *can* be true, Tim. Diane must have come out looking for us when our magnesium beacon went out so suddenly."

He turned to Mollie Blaine and the other women. "Diane Elliot is a prisoner of the Mongols," he told them simply. He looked at Mollie Blaine. "We're both in the same boat now, Mollie."

OPERATOR 5

Tears were in Mollie Blaine's eyes. "Please—forget about Gerald. Do what you can for Diane—and may God help you!"

He shook his head. "No. I'm going to keep my promise. After I've talked with Farragut, I'm riding back into the Mongol lines."

"I'm coming with you," Mollie Blaine said.

"Me, too!" Tim Donovan added.

Jimmy Christopher silently swung his horse around, led the way out of the thicket, threading a path that ran almost parallel with the Lancaster road.

TWENTY MINUTES later, they were hailed by an American sentry. And five minutes after that, Operator 5 was talking with Colonel Farragut, on the crest of Mount Misery, overlooking the American defenses.

Farragut was pale with worry and lack of sleep. "I couldn't understand your message, Operator 5," he said in short, jerky phrases. "Why should we abandon the blockhouse—"

Jimmy Christopher interrupted, telling him swiftly about the catapult towers. "A single hit by one of those catapults will bring the blockhouse down," he finished. "There!" He pointed out into the night, where the flares of the Mongol army were flickering in the first faint flush of the dawn. "See those tall towers?"

Farragut raised his glasses, peered through them for a long time. At last, he lowered them, and his hand was trembling.

"Good God, Operator 5, you're right! Those are *ballistae!* Those things will sling a half-ton rock. The blockhouses won't stand against them. We'll have to evacuate this position, or else we'll be engulfed by the Mongols!"

The half-dozen junior officers, who were standing in a small

THE COMING OF THE MONGOL HORDES

knot about them, began to stir with disappointment. They had been expecting to engage in a battle with the Mongols.

Jimmy Christopher gazed down at the feverish rush of work being carried on by Farragut's engineers. "Your men are digging trenches now?"

Farragut nodded. "I gave up the work on the blockhouse and on the breastworks when I got your message—even though I didn't understand it fully—and I set the men to work at a series of trenches along the Valley Creek Road, and up there, on the bank of the Schuylkill. But we haven't a chance of holding them. The Mongols have enough men to keep on sending wave after wave over the top. I haven't enough men to establish a decent relief reserve. I've heliographed to Philadelphia and New York for reinforcements, but there's no answer as yet...."

He paused as an orderly spurred up the hill from the heliograph station, and delivered a message. "Just in from New York, sir!"

Farragut eagerly read it, aloud.

"Colonel Farragut,
Commanding Valley Forge Encampment:

No chance of sending reinforcements from here. Purple Fleet steaming up coast toward New York Bay. We need help ourselves. For God's sake, do your best to hold Shan Hi Mung back for twenty-four hours so we can fortify Hudson River approaches to city, otherwise we'll be caught between Purple Navy and Shan Hi Mung's Mongols. Am semaphoring to Baltimore and Philadelphia for more men, but there is little hope of

OPERATOR 5

getting them. Good luck.

Lieutenant General Sylvester Ferrara,

Commanding Twenty-seventh Route Army."

Colonel Farragut dropped the sheet of paper despairingly. He laughed, with ironic bitterness. "Twenty-four hours! We'll be lucky if we can hold them for five hours!"

One of the junior officers suggested, "Couldn't we retire from this position sir, and move back on Philadelphia?"

Farragut shook his head. "This is the only place where we could stop the Mongols. They could march right around Philadelphia, to the northeast, and head straight for New York. All they'd have to do would be to leave a division as a rear guard to mop us up."

Operator 5 nodded. "That's true, Farragut."

The colonel spread his hands. "Then what'll we try—retire to New York, and let the Mongols march through here?"

"No!" Jimmy almost thundered the word. "We have to give Ferrara his twenty-four hours. I know him well enough to be sure that if he asks for that length of time, he needs it badly." He paused, then spoke the next words slowly, for greater emphasis. *"We must make our stand right here—no matter how hopeless it looks!"*

"It means," Farragut said solemnly, "that every man who stays in these trenches will be killed or captured. To sacrifice five thousand men—"

"Not five thousand," Operator 5 broke in. "It'll take five *hundred* men who are willing to die. Five hundred men who will pledge themselves to remain in the trenches and not retreat.

THE COMING OF THE MONGOL HORDES

You can throw them all into the line along the Valley Creek Road. Leave a dozen men in each of the blockhouses, to keep up a continuous rifle-fire. That'll cause the Mongols to stop and get their catapults in action. It'll take them several hours to demolish the blockhouses, because those things can only hurl one missile an hour. It takes almost an hour to load a half-ton rock into the lever, and wind up the ropes and the spring."

Jimmy Christopher was talking eagerly now, while the small group of officers listened to him with sparkling eyes. "After the Mongols demolish the blockhouses, they'll advance, thinking the battle is won. We'll have the trenches camouflaged. When the Mongols are close to the outer trench, the men will open fire. The surprise will surely drive the first wave of the enemy back. They'll retreat, re-form, and put their catapults to work on the trenches. They'll try to drop their missiles on the men in the trenches, rather than charge, at first. That may take another couple of hours." His jaws were set.

"But you want only five hundred men in the trenches," Farragut objected. "What about the other forty-five hundred?"

Jimmy smiled. "They'll split up into three groups—two of two thousand each, and one of five hundred. The two larger columns will march around, one across the Schuylkill, the other down toward Malvern. They'll attack on the right and the left flanks of the enemy. The Mongols will be taken completely by surprise, because they know that there isn't an American force in the neighborhood large enough to attempt to attack them. The two columns will try to cut through the enemy's flanks, and meet in the center of the Mongol column just behind the catapults." His eyes gleamed.

"If we can cut off those catapults from the main army, for just fifteen minutes, I'll try to capture and destroy them with the third group of five hundred!"

For a moment after Jimmy had finished outlining his daring plan, they were all silent, marveling over his audacity. Taking the offensive, against this overwhelming Mongol force, had not occurred to any of them!

Jimmy smiled tightly. "That's settled, then. I'll leave it to you, Farragut, to ask for volunteers to remain in the trenches, and for volunteers for my column of five hundred. Those will be the two most dangerous details, though none of it will be any picnic." He swung away, put a hand on Tim Donovan's shoulder. "Tim and I are going to snatch a half-hour's sleep. Wake us in thirty minutes."

HE HURRIED, with Tim, to the tent next to Mollie Blaine's, which had been assigned to them. There, they both lay down on the hard army cots. Neither had had a wink of sleep for more than forty-eight hours, but both remained wide awake now. And both were thinking the same thing. This undertaking, upon which they were venturing, might well be their last. No matter whether they were successful or not in carrying out their mad plan to seize and destroy the catapults, Diane Elliot would surely die at dawn. For they were deliberately leaving her to the tender mercies of the Mongols, in order to carry out this plan of Operator 5's.

Jimmy lay on his back on the cot, hands clasped above his

THE COMING OF THE MONGOL HORDES

head, eyes staring at the discolored canvas top of the tent. He was thinking of Diane's fresh, lovely beauty being defiled by the filthy hands of the Mongols....

He was leaving her, without making an attempt at rescue, because America needed him more. She would want it that way. But he kept telling himself that he was an unfeeling monster, unworthy of Diane Elliot's love. Otherwise, he would put aside country, duty—everything—in an effort to save her before dawn.

He turned his head, to see Tim Donovan watching him, bright-eyed, from the other cot. The boy's lips were trembling. "Jimmy, it'll be dawn soon...."

"Yes," Jimmy said harshly, "dawn!" Suddenly, he sat up on the cot. "Tim!"

The boy sat up, too. "Yes, Jimmy?"

Jimmy Christopher said slowly: "What do *you* think I ought to do? Farragut and those other officers out there think I'm inhuman—devoid of feeling. They know the Mongols have Diane. They must be wondering how I can think of strategy, and plans, with Diane slated to die at dawn. What do *you* think?"

Tim Donovan hesitated. He knew what ideals spurred on the man known as Operator 5. But he also knew that Jimmy Christopher was a warm human being, as sensitive as any man. He knew the agony of soul which Jimmy was experiencing at that moment. He did not know what his own answer should be.

"I—I don't know *what* to say, Jimmy," the boy blurted. "You've given so much to the service, you're entitled to serve yourself. But Diane is like you. She'd want you to do what you're doing now. If we knew just where she was, just what they planned to do to her, I'd say—to hell with everything, and try to get her out of it—"

He paused, as a footstep sounded outside, and the tent flap was lifted.

Mollie Blaine stood in the opening. Her face was wan and haggard. Slowly, she came into the tent, her eyes fixed on Jimmy Christopher. He arose, waiting for her to come in.

She did not speak until she had entered, dropped the flap behind her. Then she straightened her shoulders, spoke halting.

"I—I know what you're going through, Operator 5," she said. "I know you're remembering your promise about Gerald—that's one of the reasons you're heading the five hundred men who're going to attack the catapults. You're going to try to free Gerald for me."

Jimmy Christopher did not answer.

Mollie Blaine hesitated, her eyes speaking volumes of mixed emotion. "I want to release you from your promise. Never mind Gerald. Go and see what you can do for Diane. That—that's more important to you!"

Jimmy Christopher smiled at her. "Thanks, Mollie. The way things are shaping up, I can't do a thing for Diane. But I can make a try to help Gerald. I'm taking five hundred men to attack the catapults. If we're successful, we'll naturally release the prisoners. You can come along. We leave in half an hour."

Mollie stood there, her eyes widening as she grasped the fact that Operator 5 was not going to do anything to save Diane. Indignation showed in her face. But she had no opportunity to

THE COMING OF THE MONGOL HORDES

Those fierce Mongols were in full force now, ready for the test.

speak, for just then Colonel Farragut pushed his way into the tent.

He seemed to be in a hurry, and nodded curtly to Mollie Blaine. He spoke to Jimmy Christopher. "Operator 5, there's a messenger from Shan Hi Mung, at the outer breastworks, with a

OPERATOR 5

flag of truce. He has a message which he is instructed to deliver to you, personally. It—it must be about Diane!"

Jimmy nodded. "I'll come."

He went out with Farragut, and Tim motioned to Mollie Blaine. They both followed him.

Farragut explained to Jimmy, as they walked across the grounds, "It's the same messenger that was here earlier in the evening—a Captain Wai-tan, nephew of Shan Hi Mung. Those Mongols have great faith in us. Shan sends his own nephew, knowing that we won't violate a flag of truce!"

AT THE outer breastworks, Captain Lord Wai-tan was waiting, with an escort of Mongols. He bowed ironically to Jimmy, who recognized him as the same man whom he had seen, earlier in the night, riding toward the American lines with a white flag. Wai-tan spoke slowly, in English, handing to Jimmy a rolled tube of paper. "This message is from my revered uncle, the Lord Shan Hi Mung. You will no doubt not be surprised at its contents. I beg of you that you read it in private."

Jimmy took the tube, unrolled it at once. "I have no secrets from other Americans," he said quietly.

The note was short, curt—

Operator 5:

The girl, Diane Elliot, is in my hands. She will be executed at dawn, in a way that you will not like to see, unless *you* free her. You can do that by moving the American troops out of their position at Valley Forge, and leaving the road to New York open to my army. This is little enough to demand for the life

THE COMING OF THE MONGOL HORDES

of Diane Elliot, since we are assured of victory, anyway. It will merely make it easier for me. Your answer is required at once, since dawn will break by the time my messenger can return.

      Shan Hi Mung,
      Generalissimo of Purple Armies.

Jimmy Christopher held the note with steady fingers, raised his eyes to Wai-tan. "Tell me," he said, very low, "how Miss Elliot was captured."

Wai-tan bowed, smiling wickedly. "Gladly. She followed my detail, when I returned from my first trip here. We heard her horse, and ambushed her. I brought her to the carriage of my revered uncle, who was gracious enough to give her to me for an hour."

Wai-tan paused, taking an involuntary step backward at what he saw in Jimmy Christopher's eyes.

"Go on!" Jimmy said hoarsely.

Wai-tan shrugged. "But the girl is a little spit-fire. She managed to get my sword, and held it at my stomach, threatening to kill me if anyone approached. Then my uncle outwitted her. He sent an orderly to place a great stone in front of the carriage wheels. When the carriage struck the stone, it lurched sideways, and the girl was thrown off balance. The point of her sword fell away from my stomach, and we jumped upon her, capturing her once more. However, then it was too late for me to have her. Then we learned that you had escaped with your band into the American lines. So, not needing any further information from her, we decided to send you this note."

OPERATOR 5

Jimmy said softly, "I see. And this carriage of Shan Hi Mung's—it is with the army?"

"Of course. It is in the vanguard, with the catapults, which will crush your blockhouses, if you choose to resist. But if you march out and leave the road clear for us, you shall have your Elliot girl back."

There was a long moment of silence, after Wai-tan had ceased speaking.

Then, Colonel Farragut moved over to him. "We'll do it, Operator 5. We'll evacuate Valley Forge. We can dig in somewhere else—but, in the meantime, Miss Elliot will be safe once more."

Tim Donovan heard that offer of Farragut's, and he anxiously studied Jimmy Christopher's face. It was inscrutable.

At last, Operator 5 moved. Slowly, deliberately, he tore the note to shreds. "Go back and tell your master what I did with his note. And tell him, also, that if he should harm Diane Elliot, the whole world will be too small to keep him from me!"

Wai-tan blanched at the ferocity in Operator 5's tone. He took a step backward, glancing around for his men.

Jimmy went on, "As for you, Captain Lord Wai-tan, I shall settle with you. The next time I see you, without the protection of this flag of truce, I am going to kill you *with my bare hands!*"

Wai-tan grinned wolfishly. His left hand rested lightly on the curved saber at his side. The burnished mail across his broad chest shone dully in the feeble light of the growing dawn. "That will be a hard task, my American," he taunted. "I am the best

THE COMING OF THE MONGOL HORDES

swordsman in the Mongol army. You will first have to pass my saber, and after that—my hands!"

He raised his two powerful, knotted hands, and flexed his stubby fingers. "I shall be looking for you to make good your boast when the battle starts, American. I shall be behind the catapults, with my revered uncle's carriage. Come and find me!" He flung out the last challenge, as he swung on his heel toward his escort. The detail of Mongols, one of them bearing the flag of truce, fell in behind him, and marched to their horses, which were tethered some fifty feet away.

Jimmy and the others watched in silence while they mounted and rode away. That Wai-tan possessed a certain degree of courage, Jimmy Christopher was forced to admit. It took courage to come here—even under a flag of truce—and taunt an enemy in this way.

Colonel Farragut stepped up to Jimmy's side. "The man is mad! Why should he tell you of his part in the capture of Diane? He as much as told you where she's being held!"

Operator 5 smiled grimly. "He's not as foolish as you think, Farragut. There's method in his madness. He's deliberately baiting me, so that I'll come looking for him."

IT WAS growing light very quickly now, and the early morning frost chilled them all to the bone. But none thought of the cold. Now they could see clearly the vast forces of the Mongol general, spread out before Valley Forge. Two of the great catapults were directly opposite the spot where they now stood, and there was a concentration of infantry behind them, ready to move up and storm the American position as soon as the deadly *ballistae* should have finished their work. It was not yet clear enough to make out details, and Jimmy Christopher, even though he used glasses, could not locate the carriage of Shan Hi Mung.

He left Tim Donovan and Mollie Blaine here to watch the formation of the five hundred volunteers who were to go with him. Then he went back to Farragut's tent to study the plans for the morning. The movements of the three columns had to be synchronized. In Farragut's tent there were also present Captain Yarnell, who was to command the column attacking the left wing, and Major Lanstrom, in charge of the attack on the enemy's right wing. Farragut, himself, had decided to remain in the trenches.

Both Yarnell and Lanstrom reported their columns already organized, ready to go. Jimmy nodded. "You'll have to take your men across the Schuylkill, Captain," he told Yarnell. "The river is frozen, and you should be able to cross up near the old ford where Sullivan's Bridge used to be. You, Major Lanstrom, will march around the bend of Valley Creek, and take up a position on the enemy's right flank. You'll have to give Yarnell plenty of time to cross the Schuylkill and move up. In any event, don't strike until after the enemy has launched his first attack. Your signal will be a column of smoke from the top of Mount Misery."

"What about you?" Farragut asked. "Where will your five hundred men be?"

"Right in the trenches," Jimmy told him grimly. "If we turn back the first wave of the enemy attack, we'll charge, right

THE COMING OF THE MONGOL HORDES

behind them. That's our only chance of breaking the Mongol's center."

Major Lanstrom rubbed his chin with the back of his hand: "It's mad, Operator 5—the whole thing." He grinned. "And we're mad, too, for trying it. But we might as well be mad as the way we are!" He put out his hand. "See you in hell, Operator 5!"

Jimmy returned his grin, and clasped his hand. The four men shook all around. None expected to be alive at sunset. They were deliberately planning to lay down their lives so that New York should have more time to prepare its defenses.

Lanstrom and Yarnell left to take their columns away, as they needed to move at once in order to be in position when the enemy attacked.

Jimmy Christopher and Colonel Farragut pored for ten minutes over a large-scale map of the terrain opposite the American trenches. After a few moments, Jimmy raised his head. "It looks good for a swift cavalry movement. I'll mount my men for the charge. Have you got enough horses?"

Farragut nodded. "Just about. I've assigned to you the five hundred men from the Third Pennsylvania Cavalry, who were with my engineers. They're good fighters, too, and well-armed. They have pretty late-model Springfields."

"Good," said Jimmy. "And now, are there any further dispatches from Ferrara in New York?"

"Only this one," Farragut told him, lifting a sheet from his table. "It came in on the heliograph a few minutes ago."

The dispatch read—

OPERATOR 5

Colonel Farragut,
Commanding Valley Forge Encampment:

    Repeat, imperative you hold up enemy advance at Valley Forge for twenty-four hours. Heavy Purple forces marching down from Buffalo and Montreal, but neither can reach here for several days due to blocked roads and cold weather. Main force facing you is only one within marching distance able to reach us before we are prepared. Up to you. Purple Fleet lying off coast, apparently waiting for attack by land force before closing in.
                            Ferrara.

Jimmy put down the dispatch. "We *can't* fail!" he said tightly.

But even as he said it, he was thinking of Diane Elliot, a prisoner of the Mongols, slated to die in a few minutes now. He was going to fail *her*. And even if they should succeed here at Valley Forge, success would be bitter....

CHAPTER 9
THE DEVIL'S DAY

THE SUN was poking up out of the east when Jimmy Christopher stepped from Farragut's tent. A commissary wagon was unhitched at the foot of the hill, and steaming cups of hot coffee being handed out to the men who had toiled all through the night at the erection of the blockhouses and digging of trenches—and who would now go into those trenches to fight.

They were weary, shivering with the cold. Yet they joked

THE COMING OF THE MONGOL HORDES

among themselves, munching at pieces of hardtack which they dipped in the coffee.

Operator 5 and Colonel Farragut joined the line, and got their ration of coffee and hardtack. Jimmy said bitterly to Farragut, "These boys are going into battle without sleep or rest—and they'll probably die before they sleep!"

Farragut's eyes clouded. "It can't last much longer—this war. Food supplies are getting low, and men are only flesh and blood. We can't get wheat or meat. The Purple troops have cut off the eastern seaboard from all supplies. Where's it all going to end?"

"I don't know," Jimmy told him. "But I do know that America is going on with the fight until there are no more men left. If these boys have the spirit to go into battle after a night like last night, then the country isn't through!"

He glanced around at the camp. To the rear, on the parade ground, a long, low hospital tent had been erected, where doctors were treating wounded and frost-bitten men. From that tent, wagons were being loaded with these patients, to take them to the rear so as to make room for the new wounded which would be sent in from the coming battle. The blockhouse on Mount Misery, as well as that one on Mount Joy, flew the Stars and Stripes. Captain Yarnell's, and Major Lanstrom's, columns had already left. The remaining men were getting their rations and hurrying into the trenches as rapidly as possible.

Beyond the trenches, the vast host of the enemy could be plainly seen now. The catapult towers loomed above the Purple troops, their sinister shapes seeming to spell the doom of the defenders. Great rocks lay in the spoon-shaped ends of the levers. The slight breeze from the west carried to the ears of the Americans the ominous creaking of the winch-blocks which were dragging back those levers on their powerful springs.

Jimmy finished his coffee, shook hands with Farragut.

The colonel smiled. "I wish I could go with you, instead of taking command here."

Jimmy pressed his hand. "We've each got to do his job. If I fail out there, and if Yarnell and Lanstrom's columns don't break through, your position will be worse than ours."

He left the colonel, and hurried across toward the trenches. Tim Donovan and Mollie Blaine were waiting for him, the five hundred men all in their places. A low cheer went up as Jimmy appeared, and he saluted them solemnly.

Tim reported that the horses were all in readiness back of the inner-line drive.

Jimmy nodded. "Pass the word down the line, that the men are not to show themselves, and not to fire at the enemy until the Mongols charge."

The trenches were shallow affairs, hastily dug. They stretched along, parallel with Valley Creek from the Schuylkill River down past Mount Joy.

Beyond the shallow creek, which was completely frozen over, low breastworks had been thrown up, manned by sharpshooters. Those men would retire to the trenches, when the enemy attacked.

JIMMY CHRISTOPHER'S eyes sought the enemy lines. They had said that all the Americans at Valley Forge would witness the death of Diane Elliot at dawn. He was watching, a

THE COMING OF THE MONGOL HORDES

deep ache in his heart. His glasses swept the Mongol positions, and he spotted the huge, ornate carriage of Shan Hi Mung, some hundred yards behind the catapult towers. But of Diane there was no sign.

Now a deep, sinister shout went up from the Mongols. A trumpet sounded shrilly, and the men at the catapults burst into activity. Jimmy made out their figures, hauling at the ropes. There were four of those catapults, in a row, about a thousand yards from the American lines.

The one on the extreme left was the first to be fired. There was a long, high-pitched whine, and the lever sprang forward with tremendous propulsion. The huge rock was hurled into the air with terrific force, and described a wide parabola, passing over the heads of Jimmy and the men in the trenches.

It smashed into the side of Mount Misery with a tremendous crash that shook the ground, and rolled down with the force of an avalanche.

Jimmy exclaimed, "It's short! It missed the blockhouse!"

The second catapult was fired, and the rock again landed short. But the third was a direct hit. It smashed into the upper part of the structure, caving in the walls as if they had been eggshells. There was a terrible heaving and ripping of boards, and a rending, tearing crash. The blockhouse collapsed like a cardboard toy. The figures of the few Americans who had manned it could now be seen running out.

Great shouts of triumph arose from the Mongol lines, and the fourth catapult was fired. This one was aimed at the Mount Joy blockhouse. It fell far short of its target, because the catapult had been trained upon Mount Misery, and the Mongol catapulteers had had to change its position to bear south.

Two more rocks were hurled from the other catapults, but they could not reach their objective.

The Mongols worked fast, loading new heavy missiles onto the catapults. Three were being loaded with the same type of huge rocks. But some peculiar activity was going on at the fourth machine. A group of Mongol officers seemed to be gathered around the lever. Several could be seen, pushing a trussed-up object onto the spoon-shaped end.

The men in the trenches about Operator 5 watched with interest, speculating as to the nature of that object. But suddenly, Jimmy Christopher knew. He felt his blood run cold within him. He didn't need a closer look. *He knew it was Diane Elliot!*

He turned to see Tim Donovan staring out at the catapult with his field-glasses. The lad's knuckles were white with the intensity of his grip on the binoculars. He lowered them, his eyes wide with horror.

"Jimmy! That's Diane!"

Operator 5 nodded, without speaking.

"But, Jimmy—they're going to *shoot* her from the catapult! They'll hurl her through the air to smash against the blockhouse!"

JIMMY CHRISTOPHER'S brain was whirling, racing trying to think of an expedient—some means of stopping the awful thing that they were going to do with Diane.

The Mongol's idea was worthy of a brain nurtured in hell. *"All the Americans at Valley Forge will witness the execution!"* they

THE COMING OF THE MONGOL HORDES

had said. And it would truly be a spectacle—one to satisfy the sadistic lusts of Shan Hi Mung and Rudolph I, a good joke for those Mongols to chortle over at their drunken orgies.

The men in the trenches could see Diane plainly now, without the aid of glasses, because it was growing lighter. And a great shout of protest arose from them. They called to each other, frantically asking what to do.

A junior officer came running to Operator 5, along the communicating trench. "We've got to stop that, sir!" he exclaimed. "That—that's Miss Elliot they're going to shoot from the catapult. The men want to go over the top, sir—attempt to free her—"

Jimmy was standing, his eyes fixed on that catapult, hands clenched at his sides. "No, no! That's what the Mongols want. They want to get the men out in the open. They're waiting for us to lose our heads and charge. That's why they're doing that!"

"But, sir, we can't let it happen—"

"Wait!" Jimmy raised a hand. "How are the sharpshooters at the breastworks? Can they shoot well?"

"The best in the country, sir!"

"That's about a thousand-yard range," Jimmy muttered. "I wonder...."

He suddenly leaped erect, and sprang up from the trench, ran toward the breastworks in front. He fairly slid across the ice of the creek, and came running toward the sharpshooters hidden behind the breastworks. He snatched a rifle from the hands of one of the men, raised it to his shoulder. He held it there for a long minute, trying to gauge the wind, the elevation, the range. He could not afford to miss.

He waited there with the rifle at his shoulder, sighting at the little crowbar at the side of the catapult, which he had seen the Mongols pull to release the spring. A man stood at that lever, hand gripping it, apparently awaiting an order.

The rifle had telescopic sights, but Jimmy had never fired it, did not know what to allow for inaccuracy.

He heard a voice at his ear—the voice of the sharpshooter from whom he had taken the weapon. "It's absolutely accurate, sir. You don't have to worry about deflection."

Jimmy nodded thankfully. He sighted carefully, and pulled the trigger. The rifle barked, and he swiftly raised his head, heart pounding, wondering whether he had made it. A fierce surge of joy went through him, as he saw the Mongol stagger backward, release the lever, then collapse.

A shout of joy went up from the Americans. Another Mongol darted toward the lever, and Jimmy raised his rifle again. But a dozen other rifles along the line of breastworks spoke almost as one, and the second Mongol fell before he reached the lever.

"That's it, boys!" Jimmy shouted. "Keep that lever covered!"

Twice more, Mongol troopers darted toward the lever, only to die before they reached it.

JIMMY WATCHED anxiously, wondering what he should do next. It was an impossible situation. There were many Mongols on the roof of the tower, and they could easily become infuriated enough to run Diane through with their swords. It would be impossible for the marksmen here to reach those men

THE COMING OF THE MONGOL HORDES

on the roof, because of the low parapet that protected them. The situation seemed to be a stalemate.

Now he could see the Mongol troopers on the ground, going among the yoked captives who had been hauling the catapult, whipping them up.

He groaned inwardly, for he understood their strategy. They were going to move the catapult around a bit, so that the lever was hidden from the American marksmen!

Jimmy gazed at the bound figure of Diane up there. She seemed to be watching the whole thing with a detached interest. She must have given up any hope of emerging alive from this, Whatever slight bit that might have been roused in her breast, was certainly gone now.

Colonel Farragut came running up to Jimmy. "The men want to go over the top now! They don't want to wait. For God's sake, give the word. Let them at least try to save her!"

Jimmy shook his head. "No! That's what the Mongols want. Our men would be cut down by rifle-fire before they could get across!"

"But for God's sake, when they move that catapult, we won't be able to sight at the lever. Then they'll shoot her out of it!"

Suddenly, Jimmy Christopher grunted, "Hell! Look at that for guts!"

Farragut followed his glance, and at the some time a great cheer went up from the American ranks. It was a salute to pure grit. For those half-naked captives, yoked to the catapult, were *refusing* to budge! They stood still under the merciless lashes of the Mongols, and would not move an inch!

OPERATOR 5

But now the Mongols were trying to move the other three catapults into position to bear more closely on Mount Joy. The Americans yoked to those machines also refused to stir.

Farragut gulped, swallowed, and spoke. "God, we can't let those men down. I'm going to give the signal for Yarnell and Lanstrom to attack!"

Tim Donovan plucked at Operator 5's sleeve. "Go ahead, Jimmy. It's the only chance to save Diane. You've got to give her that much of a break."

Jimmy Christopher groaned. "The Mongols are waiting for us to do just that. But if the men are willing—" he waved his hand—"go ahead."

FARRAGUT WAITED for no more. He leaped up on to the trench parapet, and raised his arm in signal, waving it three times. Almost simultaneously, from the top of Mount Joy, rose a thin spiral of smoke—the signal to Yarnell and Lanstrom!

The sharpshooters at the breastworks were keeping up a continuous barrage of sniping, preventing the Mongols from reaching that lever which would send Diane Elliot hurtling to dreadful death. The Mongol troopers about the catapults were still plying their whips relentlessly—without result.

Operator 5 issued swift orders, which were relayed to the rear. In a moment, the horses of the five hundred volunteers were brought up in groups, and the men mounted, forming by squads. They were hidden from the Mongols by the breastworks in front of the trenches, so that the enemy perhaps might be taken by surprise at the first charge.

Tim Donovan and Mollie Blaine sat their mounts beside

THE COMING OF THE MONGOL HORDES

Jimmy. His eyes were still fixed anxiously on the distant figure of Diane. Now that he had decided to risk everything for her, he dreaded the thought that the sharpshooters might miss once… that one of the Mongols might finally succeed in pulling that lever.

But he tore his eyes from the catapult, turning to his men. "We're going to do just what they expect us to do. It may be that we are riding into a trap. But, for the sake of Diane Elliot—and men at New York who are depending on us—*we've got to reach those catapults!*"

The men cheered him. He turned to watch the enemy again, after instructing engineers to lay boards across the frozen creek, so that the troop might cross without danger of breaking the ice.

He waited patiently for Yarnell and Lanstrom to swing into action, in response to the signal. The Mongols had temporarily given up the attempt to reach the lever under the deadly fire of those American sharpshooters. They were concentrating upon forcing the yoked captives to move the catapults. Whips were plied, sabers flashed in the air. Many of those captives died in the next two minutes for their stubborn resistance. Jimmy shouted to the marksmen to try their luck with the Mongol overseers, and the sharpshooters began sniping at them among the captives. Several dropped, and it caused the Mongols to open fire upon the American breastworks.

A hail of lead began to pour into the sandbags which had been piled up on the other side of the creek. But little damage was done, because the men took cover firing from loopholes cut for this purpose.

A great rolling sound of musketry came from the enemy's left flank, which was not visible from this location. A moment later, firing filtered in from the right flank. Yarnell and Lanstrom had struck.

The Battle of Valley Forge was begun!

CHAPTER 10
TOWER OF TERROR

THE SOUNDS of battle on both enemy flanks grew louder and more insistent. Peering through his field glasses, Jimmy Christopher could see a busy scurrying about of Mongol officers and messengers. The enemy, no doubt, could not believe that a small force of a couple of thousand would have the audacity to attack a host of their size. They must have assumed that a large American detachment had stolen up on them in the night. Shan Hi Mung seemed to be acting in accordance with that belief. For Jimmy could see the thick masses of infantry behind the generalissimo's carriage deploying from the road, forming into marching order, and starting off to the flanks. Shan Hi Mung was depleting his forces in front of the American position to protect his flanks. That was what Jimmy had hoped for when he planned this action, and his eyes now glowed with satisfaction.

He found it hard to restrain his men, who wanted to start at once. But he kept them in hand, waiting until those thickly massed bodies of infantry had disappeared out of sight. Now there was a great gap in the road behind the carriage, for the rest of the Mongol troops had not yet come up. But they would be here shortly, of course, and it would be necessary to strike quickly.

Jimmy Christopher drew a deep breath. This was the moment. He raised his arm, shouted, "Forward, in column of fours!"

He spurred his horse forward, and picked his way over the planks across the creek, with Tim Donovan and Mollie Blaine close behind, the troop of five hundred following.

The sharpshooters had opened a passage in the breastworks, and Jimmy rode through at the head of his column. The sharpshooters, meanwhile, had spread out on either end of the breastworks. They opened a consistent, concerted fire, acting as a sort of barrage, shooting from both ends of the breastworks toward a spot in the middle, directly ahead of the point at which Jimmy's column was aiming.

The rattle of musketry filled the air as the Mongols, amazed at this sortie, answered the fire of the sharpshooters.

Operator 5, bent low in the saddle, spurred forward, with his troop spreading out in open formation behind him, making a sort of triangle of which he was the spearhead.

He rode until within a hundred yards of the enemy vanguard. Shots were whistling about him thick and fast now, but the Mongols' marksmanship was poor. In addition, they were rattled by the accurate shooting of the American sharpshooters, who increased their range, as Jimmy's column moved forward.

Operator 5 could see the catapult towers very plainly now, and, through his glasses, made out Diane's countenance as she watched the action. There was surprise in her face, and fear for these men who were throwing away their lives for the slim chance of rescuing her.

Directly ahead, Jimmy Christopher could see the yoked captives milling about the catapult, defiantly refusing to obey the frenzied orders of the Mongols who were whipping them relentlessly, slashing at them with their sabers.

Now, the charging Americans were within sixty yards.

Jimmy Christopher raised his arm, swept it forward in signal. "Charge—with bayonets!" he shouted.

Down the line behind them, the order was repeated with fierce joy, "Charge—with bayonets!"

HORSES' HOOVES drummed a deadly crescendo of martial music on the frozen turf, as the troop swung into the charge, spurring their horses forward, bayoneted guns raised on high and held in their hands like spears.

A troop of Mongol cavalry came cutting across from the south to meet them, and Jimmy, eyes blazing, headed straight for it, his column closing in behind him like the body of a lance. The Mongols galloped to meet them in wide formation, two deep, intent upon blocking their path to the catapults. But the Americans were not to be denied now. Like an avalanche, they struck that line of Mongols, and went through them without stopping, bayonets darting in and out so swiftly that the eye could not follow the flashing steel.

The Mongol horsemen broke and fled, leaving their dead on the ground. The way was clear to the catapults!

Jimmy spurred his horse on, and two companies of Mongol infantry came running into position in front of the catapults.

THE COMING OF THE MONGOL HORDES

They knelt, raising rifles. Jimmy's men would now have to charge into those rifles, at a frightful cost of human life. He had expected this, feared it. More infantry swept into position beside those two Mongol companies. It was the enemy reserves, obviously kept here for the purpose of meeting the Americans when they should come out from behind the breastworks, goaded by the sight of Diane Elliot on that catapult. But for the flank attacks which Jimmy had planned, there would have been more infantry here. However, these Mongols now constituted more than a full regiment, fully equal to mowing down the horsemen of Jimmy's troop. Even if the Americans should break through that hail of fire, certain to meet them in a moment, they would be too decimated to be a match for the infantry, in the hand-to-hand fighting which must follow.

Jimmy saw all this, but there was no retreat. He spurred forward, squarely into the teeth of those muskets, expecting every instant to feel the sting of enemy lead. The Mongols were ready to shoot, too, rifles at their shoulders, obviously waiting until the cavalry were too close to be missed.

But it was then that the diversion came.

The American captives threw off their yokes!

With a deep, angry shout, they hurled the leather yokes from them, their whip-scarred bodies rushed, barehanded, upon their guards. They swept over them, seizing their whips and weapons, trampling them under feet, as they charged down upon the rear of the kneeling Mongol infantry. Apparently, this had been a concerted move, agreed upon beforehand, for the crews of all four catapults acted in unison. Those two hundred and forty odd

OPERATOR 5

THE COMING OF THE MONGOL HORDES

Like a human tornado, Operator 5 slashed through that mêlée to the catapult ladder.

OPERATOR 5

men fell upon the rear of the Mongol troopers like a horde of avenging angels, beating with fists, slashing with whips, shooting with the weapons they had seized.

As the line of Mongol infantry bent under the onslaughts, the troopers turned to defend themselves. It was at that moment Jimmy Christopher's troop struck them.

The Mongols died like flies, under those American bayonets, and flailing hooves. Those patriots were giving no quarter today. The ex-captives were no more merciful, remembering their long hours of slavery in the yokes of the catapults, slashed backs, their fellows who had been impaled and gutted upon Mongol steel.

Within two minutes, the field around the catapult was theirs. Meantime, the American sharpshooters had come up from behind the breastworks, sending hail upon hail of lead toward the *ballista* upon which Diane Elliot was tied.

NOW, JIMMY CHRISTOPHER swung his horse around, raced for the catapult. In the distance, he could hear furious battle raging, upon both enemy flanks. Mongol trumpets were wildly summoning more troops from the rear. He could see the great carriage of Shan Hi Mung, standing behind the catapults—a hundred of the unyoked captives storming at its doors to get at the Mongol general within. But Jimmy's eyes were fixed upon the tower where Diane was tied. Sinister, overpoweringly evil, a face peered down from among those Mongol guards at the top—the lord captain, Wai-tan!

A dozen Americans had followed Jimmy toward the tower, while their comrades engaged the newly arrived forces of Mongol infantry. Jimmy was the first to reach the catapult. No

THE COMING OF THE MONGOL HORDES

Mongols were on the ground, but from the roof, several fired down. Jimmy could see one climbing out upon the immense lever to which Diane was bound. Could he kill her before being overhauled?

Jimmy leaped from his horse, jumping to the ladder which led up to the top. Two Mongols, bending over the roof's edge, instantly swung their rifles on him. They would fire, before he reached the first rung.

But the American sharpshooters, rushing up, at once realized Jimmy's purpose. Rifles raised, they sent a withering hail of led toward the roof. One Mongol shrieked, smashing to earth at Jimmy Christopher's feet. The other hastily ducked back from the roof's edge.

Jimmy seized the ladder, began to climb it. The other men mounted behind him. He gained the top, poked his head over, and a slug whined past his ear. He snapped a shot at the Mongol who had fired, saw the man stagger, and ducked just in time to avoid a hail of lead. He pushed his hand over the edge of the roof, emptying the gun at the spot where he had seen the Mongols clustered.

Taking a chance that they would be momentarily disorganized by his fire, he vaulted over the top, sinking to his knees on the roof. He saw a Mongol pointing a revolver at him, and dived low under the shot. His shoulder hit the man's knees, sent him flying, screeching with terror, over the side.

Jimmy had one fleeting glimpse of Diane Elliot, watching him from her prone position high up on the lever. Then the Mongols were upon him. They had, apparently, also emptied their guns, and it was a whirlwind of saber thrusts that assailed him.

Rolling over and over, Jimmy evaded that first rush. A dozen of his own men had also gained the roof now, and the hand-to-hand battle began, fierce, deadly.

Jimmy Christopher picked up a saber dropped by a wounded Mongol, swinging around barely in time to meet the rush of the lord captain, Wai-tan.

JIMMY RAISED his own sword, and flashed in. Wai-tan's saber slid off Jimmy's blade, harmlessly, and the Mongol's eyes gleamed with hate. He stepped back, holding his sword low. The two faced each other, forgetful of the fight raging about them here on this catapult tower roof, forgetful of the battle down below—forgetful of everything but undying hatred.

Here was the showdown.

Wai-tan's thick lips parted in a snarl. "Come and kill me with your bare hands, as you promised, American," he taunted. "But, first, pass my sword. Remember, your woman is tied up there on the catapult lever. You must work fast. Soon our main column will come up. You will be overwhelmed. Very little time remains in which to kill me with bare hands, and save your woman. I, myself, shall release the catapult spring, after our reinforcements have driven you off."

Above the shouts of the fighting men on the roof, Jimmy Christopher heard them. He knew that Wai-tan's purpose was to goad him on to a frenzied attack. But Operator 5 was too skilled a swordsman to be so easily tricked. He had studied the art of swordsmanship under the greatest masters of Europe.

THE COMING OF THE MONGOL HORDES

Many times he had used sword and the saber when his own life, and the lives of others, depended upon his skill. Yet always he remembered the prime lesson of fighting with blades—he who loses his head, loses his life.

He circled Wai-tan warily. Then suddenly, using the saber like a fencing foil, his blade darted in and out—and a raw gash showed on Wai-tan's cheek. Blood trickled from the cut. It had been only a touch, not a frenzied rush.

Wai-tan glowered, and thrust. Jimmy parried, skillfully. There was still no chance for the thing he wanted to do, but he was making that chance. Once more he thrust lightly, and this time his point darted in between the corselet and the chain-mail of Wai-tan's sleeves. It was just another prick, but it served to infuriate the Mongol. He snarled, leaped in, his blade slashing down for a killing blow. Jimmy smiled. It was what he had expected—wanted. His own saber glinted in the sun, as he parried the mad slash, twisted his wrist, and jerked backward. The blade flew from Wai-tan's hand—he was disarmed!

For a moment, the Mongol captain stood there stupidly, uncomprehending. The *coup* had been so swift, so unexpected, that he was unable to believe that he did not still hold his sword. Now, for the first time, a twinge of fear showed across his brutal countenance. He backed away from Jimmy's flashing sword.

Operator 5 did not press his advantage. He dropped the sword, advanced toward the other, without a weapon.

"Now, Wai-tan," he said bleakly, "I shall kill you with my bare hands!"

The Mongol regained his courage. His eyes scanned Jimmy

OPERATOR 5

Christopher's slight build, speedily comparing it with his own. Operator 5's appearance was deceptive. Every ounce of him was bone, hardened muscle. He had lived through privations which would have killed the average man, but which had simply toughened him to a point almost beyond belief. Yet it did not show on him.

Wai-tan's thick lips spread in a smile that told of the return of his courage. He crouched, spread his hands like a wrestler. This man, he thought, was an utter fool. He would finish him, easily.

Jimmy advanced squarely upon him, and Wai-tan suddenly straightened, raised his foot in a smashing kick. It was a deadly *savate,* used by fighters who fight with no holds barred. But Operator 5 had learned rough-and-tumble combat in a hard school. He had read Wai-tan's intention in his small pig-eyes, was ready for it. His slim, supple figure twisted to one side, and the Mongol's foot merely slashed at empty air. But in the next instant Jimmy's hand had gripped his ankle, and was yanking him forward.

Wai-tan lost his balance, sprawled, clawing at the air. Jimmy stepped in close, seized him by the collar, kept him from falling. His right fist, knotted into a hard ball, smashed into Wai-tan's face, crashing full against the man's nose.

Wai-tan screamed, flailing his fists Again and again, Jimmy Christopher struck, smashing that evil face to a pulp. Wai-tan's big hands went searching for Jimmy's throat, but Jimmy let him go. He almost fell, recovered his balance, let out a mad bull roar, and charged across at Operator 5.

Jimmy's eyes were now cold, merciless. He waited until

THE COMING OF THE MONGOL HORDES

Wai-tan was almost upon him, then side-stepped with the speed of the trained boxer. Wai-tan kept going under his own impetus, uttered a piercing shriek as he realized he was heading toward the roof's edge. Again and again, he screamed, and suddenly his foot caught in the low parapet, tripping him, as he went hurtling off the tower to the accompaniment of a scream of mad terror.

Jimmy Christopher stood still, as his ears heard that sickening crash below. It was the end of the lord captain Wai-tan....

JIMMY TURNED to survey the fight on the roof. The Americans were mastering the Mongols. On the other catapults, other Americans had succeeded in climbing to the roof, and capturing them. The *ballistae* were in American hands.

Operator 5 climbed out upon the long lever, reaching Diane's side. Their eyes met, and they smiled, but neither said one word to the other. Words would have been utterly superfluous at that moment.

Jimmy Christopher rested precariously on the beam, and, while the battle raged below them, he leaned over and pressed his lips to hers. She met his kiss ardently, their lips expressing far more than words could ever have done. Then, with the saber which he had picked up again, he severed the cords holding her wrists, helped her down along the beam, toward the roof of the tower.

Only then did she speak. "Darling," she whispered, "I had never hoped to see you again!"

His arm was around her slim waist, as she tried to pin together her blouse, which had been ripped wide in front by Wai-tan's thick fingers.

OPERATOR 5

Now the other Americans on the tower roof, having overcome the Mongols, crowded about them, showering congratulations.

Jimmy Christopher turned his eyes from Wai-tan's smashed body below to study the battle.

Yarnell's column was marching in from the left to meet Major Lanstrom's command which was coming in from the right. They had fought their way through the Mongol opposition. On the immediate field, the ground belonged to the Americans. Colonel Farragut was down below, consolidating their position.

But as Operator 5 peered along the Lancaster road, to the west, his forehead wrinkled in a frown. Thick clouds of dust were rising from the road. That meant the main body of the Mongol infantry was moving up to the attack. They would outnumber the Americans, twenty to one—and their system was to attack in thick mass formation, then overwhelming all resistance. In less than twenty minutes they would arrive, bearing down upon this decimated American force, already so exhausted and wearied by the battle just fought.

Grimly, Jimmy Christopher made his way down to the ground, followed by Diane Elliot.

Colonel Farragut met him at the bottom. With Farragut were Tim Donovan, and Mollie Blaine—a very happy Mollie Blaine, for she was resting her golden hair upon the shoulder of a half-naked man whose back was scarred by lash strokes.

"My husband," she murmured. "Gerald led that revolt of the captives."

Jimmy shook Gerald Blaine's hand, warmly. "If it hadn't been

THE COMING OF THE MONGOL HORDES

for you," he said, "our charge would have failed. I wish you every happiness."

Mollie Blaine and Diane Elliot came into each other's arms, with wet eyes. "I don't think there are two happier women in the world," Mollie Blaine was saying.

But Colonel Farragut drew Jimmy Christopher aside. "This is all very well," he said. "But what about that Mongol army marching upon us? We can't stand against them."

Strangely enough, Jimmy Christopher did not seem greatly concerned about that threat. "What happened to Shan Hi Mung?" he asked.

"Shan escaped, with Rudolph and some woman," Farragut told him. "I caught a glimpse of their party riding like hell to meet the main army. We were too busy to stop them."

Now they were surrounded by a bevy of junior officers, all rejoicing at the victory. Yet, in the eyes of each, was that cloud of anxiety. What had Operator 5 planned to do about the approaching Mongol host?

Farragut voiced their worry, repeating his question. "What are we going to do now, Operator 5? We can't stand against Shan's whole army—"

Jimmy Christopher smiled, enigmatically. "We have victory in our hands, Farragut!" He pointed to the four catapult towers. "Load them with rocks. The Mongols are marching in close formation. Do you know what one of those rocks will do to infantry in close formation?"

Farragut's eyes sparkled. "By God, Operator 5, you've hit it! Let's go now!" Jimmy went on swiftly, "We'll form our men in

OPERATOR 5

open formation, in front of the catapults, to repel any charge. And we'll blast the enemy off the road!"

Farragut turned, immediately transformed into a dynamo of energy. His curt, staccato orders sent soldiers scurrying for huge boulders, the cavalry into reserve behind the breastworks, and placed the unmounted men at digging hasty trenches around the catapults.

Twenty minutes later, when the close-packed hosts of the Mongols came in sight, the deadly catapults hurled death and destruction into the ranks of their former owners. The Mongol army was hurled back upon itself in wildest possible confusion....

THE REST of the Battle of Valley Forge is history. It is well known how the Americans, elated at their success, engaged in a sortie that night, which drove the Mongols back a mile. The American position at Valley Forge was held for ten days instead of twenty-four hours!

Only when that urgent heliograph signal came from General Ferrara at New York, did the Americans evacuate Valley Forge. That message, on the evening of the tenth day, read—

> Operator 5:
>
> Have completed defenses of Hudson River approaches. We can hold the city against Shan Hi Mung. But Purple fleet is sailing into lower bay to bombard us. If fleet gets range of our Hudson River defenses, they can demolish them and leave way clear for Shan Hi Mung. Need your presence urgently.
>
> Ferrara.

THE COMING OF THE MONGOL HORDES

Jimmy read the telegram, and put it down, facing the small group assembled around him. There was Colonel Farragut, Diane Elliot, Tim Donovan, Mollie and Gerald Blaine, as well as a group of officers.

"Gentlemen," Jimmy said, "it looks as if we now move to New York."

Approving nods, from around the table, greeted this.

"God will yet grant America freedom!" said Operator 5.*

---

* AUTHOR'S NOTE: Most people, who have not made a careful study of the Purple Invasion, are inclined to think that the most trying days of this period ended when the power of Emperor Rudolph in the United States was smashed for the first time. That this view is entirely erroneous is proved by the following excerpt from Harrison Stievers' monumental history of the Purple Wars: "*After the Battle of Valley Forge, the real crisis bore down upon America. When Rudolph I once more regained command of his vast war machine, America was faced by an adversary doubly venomous because of his previous disgrace. The siege of New York was only a prelude to the months of dread which loomed before our people.*"

It is with the next phase of the Purple Wars that the forthcoming novel will deal.

POPULAR HERO PULPS AVAILABLE NOW:

THE SPIDER
- ❏ #1: The Spider Strikes — $13.95
- ❏ #2: The Wheel of Death — $13.95
- ❏ #3: Wings of the Black Death — $13.95
- ❏ #4: City of Flaming Shadows — $13.95
- ❏ #5: Empire of Doom! — $13.95
- ❏ #6: Citadel of Hell — $13.95
- ❏ #7: The Serpent of Destruction — $13.95
- ❏ #8: The Mad Horde — $13.95
- ❏ #9: Satan's Death Blast — $13.95
- ❏ #10: The Corpse Cargo — $13.95
- ❏ #11: Prince of the Red Looters — $13.95
- ❏ #12: Reign of the Silver Terror — $13.95
- ❏ #13: Builders of the Dark Empire — $13.95
- ❏ #14: Death's Crimson Juggernaut — $13.95
- ❏ #15: The Red Death Rain — $13.95
- ❏ #16: The City Destroyer — $13.95
- ❏ #17: The Pain Emperor — $13.95
- ❏ #18: The Flame Master — $13.95
- ❏ #19: Slaves of the Crime Master — $13.95
- ❏ #20: Reign of the Death Fiddler — $13.95
- ❏ #21: Hordes of the Red Butcher — $13.95
- ❏ #22: Dragon Lord of the Underworld — $13.95
- ❏ #23: Master of the Death-Madness — $13.95
- ❏ #24: King of the Red Killers — $13.95
- ❏ #25: Overlord of the Damned — $13.95
- ❏ #26: Death Reign of the Vampire King — $13.95
- ❏ #27: Emperor of the Yellow Death — $13.95
- ❏ #28: The Mayor of Hell — $13.95
- ❏ #29: Slaves of the Murder Syndicate — $13.95
- ❏ #30: Green Globes of Death — $13.95
- ❏ #31: The Cholera King — $13.95
- ❏ #32: Slaves of the Dragon — $13.95
- ❏ #33: Legions of Madness — $12.95
- ❏ #34: Laboratory of the Damned — $12.95
- ❏ #35: Satan's Sightless Legion — $12.95
- ❏ #36: The Coming of the Terror — $12.95
- ❏ #37: The Devil's Death-Dwarfs — $12.95
- ❏ #38: City of Dreadful Night — $12.95
- ❏ #39: Reign of the Snake Men — $12.95
- ❏ #40: Dictator of the Damned — $12.95
- ❏ #41: The Mill-Town Massacres — $12.95
- ❏ #42: Satan's Workshop — $12.95
- ❏ #43: Scourge of the Yellow Fangs — $12.95
- ❏ #44: The Devil's Pawnbroker — $12.95
- ❏ #45: Voyage of the Coffin Ship — $12.95
- ❏ #46: The Man Who Ruled in Hell — $13.95
- ❏ #47: Slaves of the Black Monarch — $13.95
- ❏ #48: Machineguns Over the White House — $13.95
- ❏ #49: The City That Dared Not Eat — $13.95
- ❏ #50: Master of the Flaming Horde — $13.95
- ❏ #51: Satan's Switchboard — $13.95
- ❏ #52: Legions of the Accursed Light — $13.95
- ❏ #53: The City of Lost Men — $13.95
- ❏ #54: The Grey Horde Creeps — $13.95
- ❏ #55: City of Whispering Death — $13.95
- ❏ #56: When Thousands Slept in Hell — $13.95
- ❏ #57: Satan's Shakles — $14.95
- ❏ #58: The Emperor From Hell — $14.95
- ❏ #59: The Devil's Candlesticks — $14.95
- ❏ #60: The City That Paid to Die — $14.95
- ❏ #61: The Spider at Bay — $14.95
- ❏ #62: Scourge of the Black Legions — $14.95
- ❏ #63: The Withering Death — $14.95
- ❏ #64: Claws of the Golden Dragon — $14.95
- ❏ #65: The Song of Death — $14.95
- ❏ #66: The Silver Death Reign — $14.95
- ❏ **NEW:** #67: Blight of the Blazing Eye — $14.95

THE WESTERN RAIDER
- ❏ #1: Guns of the Damned — $13.95
- ❏ #2: The Hawk Rides Back from Death — $13.95
- ❏ #3: Gun-Call for the Lost Legion — $13.95
- ❏ #4: The Law of Silver Trent — $13.95
- ❏ #5: The Gun-Prayer of Silver Trent — $13.95
- ❏ #6: Silver Trent Rides Alone — $13.95

G-8 AND HIS BATTLE ACES
- ❏ #1: The Bat Staffel — $13.95

CAPTAIN SATAN
- ❏ #1: The Mask of the Damned — $13.95
- ❏ #2: Parole for the Dead — $13.95
- ❏ #3: The Dead Man Express — $13.95
- ❏ #4: A Ghost Rides the Dawn — $13.95
- ❏ #5: The Ambassador From Hell — $13.95

DR. YEN SIN
- ❏ #1: Mystery of the Dragon's Shadow — $12.95
- ❏ #2: Mystery of the Golden Skull — $12.95
- ❏ #3: Mystery of the Singing Mummies — $12.95

POPULAR HERO PULPS AVAILABLE NOW:

ACE G-MAN
- ❏ #1: The Suicide Squad Reports for Death — $14.95
- ❏ #2: Coffins for the Suicide Squad — $14.95
- ❏ #3: Shells for the Suicide Squad — $14.95
- ❏ #4: The Suicide Squad in Corpse-Town — $14.95
- ❏ #5: Wanted–In Three Pine Coffins — $14.95

OPERATOR 5
- ❏ #1: The Masked Invasion — $13.95
- ❏ #2: The Invisible Empire — $13.95
- ❏ #3: The Yellow Scourge — $13.95
- ❏ #4: The Melting Death — $13.95
- ❏ #5: Cavern of the Damned — $13.95
- ❏ #6: Master of Broken Men — $13.95
- ❏ #7: Invasion of the Dark Legions — $13.95
- ❏ #8: The Green Death Mists — $13.95
- ❏ #9: Legions of Starvation — $13.95
- ❏ #10: The Red Invader — $13.95
- ❏ #11: The League of War-Monsters — $13.95
- ❏ #12: The Army of the Dead — $13.95
- ❏ #13: March of the Flame Marauders — $13.95
- ❏ #14: Blood Reign of the Dictator — $13.95
- ❏ #15: Invasion of the Yellow Warlords — $13.95
- ❏ #16: Legions of the Death Master — $13.95
- ❏ #17: Hosts of the Flaming Death — $13.95
- ❏ #18: Invasion of the Crimson Death Cult — $13.95
- ❏ #19: Attack of the Blizzard Men — $13.95
- ❏ #20: Scourge of the Invisible Death — $13.95
- ❏ #21: Raiders of the Red Death — $13.95
- ❏ #22: War-Dogs of the Green Destroyer — $13.95
- ❏ #23: Rockets From Hell — $13.95
- ❏ #24: War-Masters from the Orient — $13.95
- ❏ #25: Crime's Reign of Terror — $13.95
- ❏ #26: Death's Ragged Army — $13.95
- ❏ #27: Patriots' Death Battalion — $13.95
- ❏ #28: The Bloody Forty-five Days — $13.95
- ❏ #29: America's Plague Battalions — $13.95
- ❏ #30: Liberty's Suicide Legions — $13.95
- ❏ #31: Siege of the Thousand Patriots — $13.95
- ❏ #32: Patriots' Death March — $14.95
- ❏ #33: Revolt of the Lost Legions — $14.95
- ❏ #34: Drums of Destruction — $14.95
- ❏ #35: The Army Without a Country — $14.95
- ❏ #36: The Bloody Frontiers — $14.95
- ❏ **NEW:** #37: The Coming of the Mongol Hordes — $14.95

CAPTAIN COMBAT
- ❏ #1: The Sky Beast of Berlin — $13.95
- ❏ #2: Red Wings For the Blood Battalion — $13.95
- ❏ #3: Low Ceiling For Nazi Hell Hawks — $13.95

DUSTY AYRES AND HIS BATTLE BIRDS
- ❏ #1: Black Lightning! — $13.95
- ❏ #2: Crimson Doom — $13.95
- ❏ #3: The Purple Tornado — $13.95
- ❏ #4: The Screaming Eye — $13.95
- ❏ #5: The Green Thunderbolt — $13.95
- ❏ #6: The Red Destroyer — $13.95
- ❏ #7: The White Death — $13.95
- ❏ #8: The Black Avenger — $13.95
- ❏ #9: The Silver Typhoon — $13.95
- ❏ #10: The Troposphere F-S — $13.95
- ❏ #11: The Blue Cyclone — $13.95
- ❏ #12: The Tesla Raiders — $13.95

MAVERICKS
- ❏ #1: Five Against the Law — $12.95
- ❏ #2: Mesquite Manhunters — $12.95
- ❏ #3: Bait for the Lobo Pack — $12.95
- ❏ #4: Doc Grimson's Outlaw Posse — $12.95
- ❏ #5: Charlie Parr's Gunsmoke Cure — $12.95

THE MYSTERIOUS WU FANG
- ❏ #1: The Case of the Six Coffins — $12.95
- ❏ #2: The Case of the Scarlet Feather — $12.95
- ❏ #3: The Case of the Yellow Mask — $12.95
- ❏ #4: The Case of the Suicide Tomb — $12.95
- ❏ #5: The Case of the Green Death — $12.95
- ❏ #6: The Case of the Black Lotus — $12.95
- ❏ #7: The Case of the Hidden Scourge — $12.95

THE SECRET 6
- ❏ #1: The Red Shadow — $13.95
- ❏ #2: House of Walking Corpses — $13.95
- ❏ #3: The Monster Murders — $13.95
- ❏ #4: The Golden Alligator — $13.95

CAPTAIN ZERO
- ❏ #1: City of Deadly Sleep — $13.95
- ❏ #2: The Mark of Zero! — $13.95
- ❏ #3: The Golden Murder Syndicate — $13.95

www.ingramcontent.com/pod-product-compliance
Ingram Content Group UK Ltd.
Pitfield, Milton Keynes, MK11 3LW, UK
UKHW011410290825
7643UKWH00008B/24